You ~~enemy, but you know the soldier sure is. You take care-~~ful aim, pull the trigger, and blam! The guard falls back, knocked out cold with your first shot.

Zygash snarls and fires at you! His first shot hits a barrel, yet it hurts as though it actually hit you. Your best friend is now your enemy.

You can't escape. You must decide whether to fire on Gash; he's firing on you!

If you fire at Gash, go to 54.
If you try to reason with him, go to 51.

The decisions are yours as you battle for freedom in *The Galactic Challenge!*

Endless Quest® BOOKS

Endless Quest® BOOKS

Galactic Challenge

Allen Varney

GALACTIC CHALLENGE

Copyright ©1995 TSR, Inc.
All Rights Reserved.

Random House and its affiliate companies have worldwide distribution rights in the book trade for English language products of TSR, Inc.

Distributed to the book and hobby trade in the United Kingdom by TSR Ltd.

Distributed to the toy and hobby trade by regional distributors.

Cover model by Dennis Kauth. Interior art by Terry Dykstra.

First Printing: July 1995
Printed in the United States of America.
Library of Congress Catalog Card Number: 94-68143
9 8 7 6 5 4 3 2 1

ISBN: 0-7869-0158-6

TSR, Inc.
201 Sheridan Springs Road
Lake Geneva, WI 53147
United States of America

TSR Ltd.
120 Church End, Cherry Hinton
Cambridge CB1 3LB
United Kingdom

In this book, set in our galaxy in the far future, you are space pirate Rogan Hayl. Yes, *the* Rogan Hayl, marksmanship medalist (Amarak II Blaster, human division) in the Morione Domain's Officer Training Academy, just before you were dishonorably discharged for "rebellious conduct."

The Rogan Hayl who won the Laestre Sector Trans-Stellar Grand Prix three times running, always under assumed names—because every Domain officer in the sector had warrants for your arrest.

The same Rogan Hayl who stole the Akinasian Silver Vortex out of the palace vault on Wyze; who, eluding every cruiser in Kellinon Sector, delivered the Vortex across the Domain to its rightful owners on Akinas; who accepted a stingy reward from the planetary baron, smiled, and later stole the baron's priceless personal collection of Babannian mood crystals.

That Rogan Hayl.

For years you smuggled contraband past the bureaucrats of that star-spanning empire, the Morione

Domain. You raced circles around their patrol ships in your souped-up G12 Marauder XX spacecraft, the *Prosperogenesis*. Your copilot and best friend was Zygash, one of the scaly four-armed giants of the alien race called the G'rax. You and Gash poured all your profit into improving the *Prosperogenesis*, and now she's the fastest craft in space. At least, you hope so.

People on a hundred worlds could spot you—a strong, handsome smuggler with black hair, glittering eyes, and a smooth tongue. You favor black trousers, high boots of Carelaxian leather, and roomy white shirts. And, of course, a well-oiled blaster holster.

Smuggling eventually got tougher as the Morione Domain grew more powerful and brutal. The Domain has made innocent people's lives hard everywhere.

Led by the tyrant emperor, Darenon Morione, the Elite Imperial Soldiers terrorize the races of a hundred worlds. The Domain's corrupt bureaucracy creates endless petty laws that only it can understand. Then it enforces them as it desires, declaring its enemies criminals.

The Domain is governed by scions of the clans, the great ruling families who control every sector. Some of the clan houses rule dozens of planetary systems, always with an iron hand.

Against the Morione Domain stands the Resistance. Years ago a few brave rebels faced down the Domain on two or three worlds. Soon the Resistance controlled several worlds and spread rapidly, gaining support from the public everywhere.

You chose the good fight. You've served the Resistance well so far, and you like it a lot better than the Domain academy. Looser, less structured, lots of sneak attacks—that's more your style!

This adventure reads just like a book—but you'll determine its direction. As you read, you'll be asked to make choices. The paths you choose will directly affect the story's outcome. So choose wisely.

Go right on to 1.

1

You and Gash have taken the *Genesis* to the planet Silverlight, just beyond the border of Carabajal Sector, to pick up supplies for the Resistance. "Hey, Gash!" you call as you enter the hangar bay. "I got the stabilizers, but can you believe that thief Bellor wanted five hundred credits for an ordinary—?" You stop.

Zygash and the *Prosperogenesis* are gone. You left for only a short while, but that was time enough for a sudden blast-off. You can still smell the burnt fuel in the air and see the fresh scorches on the far wall. Tools and lifters were thrown everywhere by the blast.

There's no one around but a maintenance robot, a humanoid metal figure about waist high. It walks jerkily over to a disposal chute to discard the trash it holds in its pincers. "You, bot!" you call. "Where's my friend and my ship?"

"The scaly pilot launched a few moments ago," the robot replies in a deep mechanical voice. "Created quite a mess, too, but of course it's my job to clean it up." This is an MRP 946-X ("Merpie") unit, a repair and cleanup model found in nearly all spaceports. You remember that its name is Wrench.

"Where did he go, Wrench? Why? When will he be back?"

"If I understood right, he said he was off to join the Morione Domain and help destroy the Resistance."

"*What?*"

"He started by demolishing a bunch of skimmers and spacecraft out on the launch field. I suppose those were Resistance ships. Good shot. I'll have my repair work cut out for me. Inasmuch as he took all the power cores and food stocks, I imagine he plans not to return. However, he did leave a message for you."

Shocked by the overwhelming destruction, you almost miss the robot's last words. "A message? Gash left a message for me?"

"Yes, sir. Here, it's on this readout."

The robot wheels over and hands you a small hand-held data display unit. You touch a button and Zygash's face appears on the tiny screen: round, lizardlike, with purple scales, heavy brow ridges, and a wide mouth full of pointed teeth. "*Hnnnaraaagh hnaagh nghuuhngg*," says the G'rax.

"What do you mean, 'Long live the Domain'?" you say to Gash—shout to him, actually. But you're not talking to Gash, you're only listening to his recording.

Gash's face dissolves to another, a human male who looks about thirty years old. Except—his black eyes look older, and there's something strange about his skin. A mask? The man looks vaguely familiar.

"A message for Captain Rogan Hayl of the Resistance," he says. "I have recruited your longtime friend, the G'rax known as Zygash, to serve Clan Carabajal and the Morione Domain. The G'rax has brought with him your refitted smuggler's vessel, the *Prosperogenesis*. These are the first fruits of my new weapon, the Subverter. With the Subverter I can reach across space and turn any mind to the Domain's cause. I have begun by subverting the G'rax."

Now you recognize the face—it's Duke Carabajal, the leader of the scion family of Carabajal, the rulers of this space sector. You've seen his picture in Resistance briefings, because he's a cruel dictator and a sworn enemy of the Resistance. But he looked much older before, and in holo-tape recordings he sounded hesitant and confused. Here, in this recording you hold, Duke Carabajal looks young and sounds vigorous. How did he do it?

Carabajal's recorded voice continues. "Captain Hayl, listen carefully. Report immediately to the central Domain administration building here on Silverlight. Turn yourself in to the watch commander; he will arrange your transport to my Chateau-Station orbiting the planet Bryson. If you do not comply, you will never see your friend or your ship again."

The data readout grows warm in your hand. Wrench the robot says, "Captain Hayl, I'm reading a strong power buildup—"

Before the robot finishes speaking, you throw the readout across the hangar bay and dive for the floor. But you needn't have worried. The readout's explosion is surprisingly small, just a sharp *bang!*

You think, There goes any evidence. As you run to find the nearest dispatch officer, you try to remember when you last saw Zygash. A short time ago, the G'rax seemed normal. He was griping about the spaceport facilities on this outpost planet, but he gripes about every spaceport. Could this new Domain weapon really have worked so suddenly?

In a crowded hallway before a large viewing window you find your old friend Owen, a ship dispatch officer and secret member of the Resistance. He and the crowd watch the flames of ship fires across the spaceport tarmac.

"Owen, what happened?"

"Hayl!" Owen cries, surprised and furious. "You have the nerve to stick around here after your partner blows up half the port!"

"Owen, listen. The Domain has taken over Gash's mind with a new weapon called the Subverter. I got the story from Duke Carabajal himself. He left a recording, but it blew up."

Owen looks blank. "You expect me to believe that?"

You almost slug him. "Yes! If I wanted to lie, don't you think I could do better than that?"

Owen draws you away from the crowd. "Listen, Hayl. Much as I'd like to believe you and Duke Carabajal just shared a pleasant chat about some new superweapon, there are lots of people who won't. Zygash has just destroyed the entire Resistance fleet on Silverlight. Witnesses saw the *Genesis* lift without permission. They heard the G'rax raving on the ship radio, saying he'd wreck the Resistance. They saw him strafe the ships, then head for the Domain docking station in orbit. And you can see the fires as well as I can." By now the ships are totally burned. "The easiest explanation is that your scaly friend has gone over."

"Owen, everyone here knows Gash would never join the Domain!"

"A well-reasoned argument," says Owen drily. "Can you explain why the Domain would pick Gash as its first target for this weapon? Or why Carabajal would leave a message for you, explaining what he'd done?"

You have no answer but a scowl.

Owen sighs. "You can tell the commanders about this Subverter story. They won't believe you, but at least they probably won't lock you up. If you're still with us, we'll have to write off Zygash and salvage what ships we can. Then—"

"I'm still with you, but nobody's writing off Gash! I'll find him and the *Genesis* and see what happened."

Leaving Owen standing, you hop on a passing hallway shuttle and head for the spaceport exit.

Duke Carabajal wants you at the Domain headquarters, but you never think for a second of following his order. That would betray everyone you know in the Resistance. Instead, you start tracking Zygash and the *Prosperogenesis*.

You find the Domain ship departure registry in an obscure building downtown. Once the building housed stores offering Travilian glowglass, fruits of the millennium, trees of Fornax, and brilliant Rashymian rugs of webweaver silk.

Now the building stands deserted. The Domain hounded the merchants along this avenue out of business, for it believed the stores harbored Resistance spies tapping into the registry's datalink. But the merchants were innocent. The Domain didn't know that Resistance spies had obtained high-clearance security codes that let you tap into any datalink.

The ship departure registry is strikingly small, one room with a data-bank hookup and a few announcement screens. Looks like it used to be a public recreation room in the old days. You can still see the holo hookups and hi-slide braces. But under the Domain's rule, it's just a barren room. At least there are no guards around. You talk to the data bank.

The Domain docking facility records show that a ship transfer took place earlier today. Two facts catch your attention.

A modified G12 Marauder XX, clearly the *Prosperogenesis*, was flown by robot pilot to the Domain's mining colony of Dvaad, an asteroid in the Dalorvan Minor system.

The pilot of the freighter, a G'rax, remained on Silverlight's orbital docking station when the ship left for Dvaad. The G'rax then took the next Domain shuttle to Pellaj, a waterworld in the same system as Dvaad. Pellaj, Pellaj. You don't remember much there but a seawater distillation operation, a floating stronghold run by the Domain governor Baron Jorth.

Now you've learned not one, but two destinations:

Pellaj and Dvaad.

An announcement on a nearby screen catches your notice. A miner, Jaspon Dentoze, is looking for a passenger to Dvaad, the asteroid mine. There's no mention of fare, but you know of many miners who carry passengers for free, just to pass the time on long journeys.

You have nothing else to do here. You have to find Zygash and the *Genesis* so you can clear your friend's name and get your ship back. But first you want to look into his departure; second, you have to find another ship to follow him.

You can think of two sources for clues:

Kregg, a sleazy but knowledgeable informant, hangs out in the Hotjets bar near the Silverlight spaceport. He might have heard something, though he's hardly trustworthy.

The Resistance base near the spaceport is probably safe. The Resistance guerrillas may be able to get you a ship, if they have any left, and possibly some information. You wonder if you're welcome there now. Where will you go first?

If you visit Kregg the stoolie, go to 13.
If you visit the Resistance base, go to 15.
If you want to leave the planet Silverlight, go to 45.

2

After a frightening launch from Silverlight, you wonder how the *Rustbucket* made it to orbit—and when was the last time it got here—and where is the pilot that flew it. You don't want to guess at that last question, but the shaky life-support system gives all too many clues. You swear you can hear the thin whine of a pressure leak.

But the thing has held together so far as you head into blackness toward the center of Silverlight's system. The only way this inertial eDrive unit can make a jump is with a speed-boost. And the only way to get that boost is to slingshot around the gravity well of Silverlight's primary star, the sun that provides this system with heat and light.

Approaching the primary, you pick up speed as its gravity clutches at the ship. Bigger than ten thousand worlds, it looms ever larger in the front viewport. You check and recheck your course figures, hoping you didn't misplace a decimal.

Larger. Almost time.

Movement out the right viewport catches your eye. Coronals! The living creatures that inhabit the corona, the hot vacuum around every star. Where most life-forms are matter suspended in a liquid, like water in human beings, the coronals are plasma shaped by intense magnetic fields. Shapeless flickers of light, they dance in circles and somersaults, at play endlessly.

Even at this tense moment, you steal a glance at these rarely-seen beings. A good thing, too, because you notice you're barreling down on one in the *Rustbucket*!

You swerve wildly. When you recover your bearings, the view ahead is clear. You're not sure if you got out of its way, or if the coronal got out of yours, but your fast wingover must have helped avoid collision. However, the *Rustbucket* groans in protest at the sudden maneuver. You murmur, "Don't desert me now, love," your pet phrase in the cockpit of the *Prosperogenesis*.

But this isn't the *Genesis*, and the *Rustbucket* seems quite willing to desert you. Alarms squeal, the superstructure shakes, and for one terrible instant you lurch as the gravity blinks out.

The worst is still to come. Now the *Rustbucket* is

falling to pieces, and you're close enough to Silverlight's primary to feel the starshine on your skin.

"Captain Hayl, I believe we're about to be horribly vaporized," says Wrench.

"I know, you—!" You have no time to curse. The maintenance robot might save your life. But this ship might be so old that Wrench doesn't know how to fix it. Then its repairs would make things worse. Will you ask Wrench to repair the ship?

If you want Wrench to help, go to 11.
If you don't want Wrench to help, go to 20.

3

This old scow may not win races, but it's no junkheap. You slide in behind the control console and run through the emergency launch sequence. The engines grumble like tired crewmen, their noise almost lost amid the louder rumbling from the sinking stronghold. "Come on, guy," you whisper to the ship, trying to rush what can never be rushed. Gash squeezes into the copilot seat, and you feel better.

The launch deck tilts beneath the ship, threatening to flip it onto its back. But you hit the thrusters just in time, and the freighter spills into the air. Climbing upward, you see the deck below crack into pieces.

You also see something else—another blast trail! A powerful space-yacht, a high-speed starcruiser with streamlined contours, zooms toward orbit, passing you without effort.

"*Gnnnraaaarrrhh!*" howls Gash, but you already know whose ship it is.

Your own ship labors upward, finally reaching orbit. Pellaj is a blue sphere below, frosted with clouds. From here it seems unharmed by the ravages of the Domain's destroyed stronghold. From here it's peaceful, quiet—

"Hayl!" cries a voice over the freighter's radio. "You have destroyed my stronghold. Now I shall destroy you!" Baron Jorth's yacht soars into view, blaster cannons firing.

Jerking the controls hard over, you try to evade the blasts. You coax more out of the freighter than its designers dreamed possible. First you sweep out of Jorth's line of fire with a barrel roll, and then an arching half-roll and turn bring you around over the yacht. Perhaps dumbstruck by your brilliant piloting, Jorth takes his time in turning to follow.

"No good," you tell Gash. "We're just fighting a delaying action. A crate like this can't stall that yacht for long. Think you can plan the jump to eSpace?"

"*Hnnr.*"

You sigh. You beat on the controls. This clunky freighter handles like an obsolete aircar. When the lights blink out and the ship shakes from a blaster hit, you're hardly surprised.

The freighter's shields were never designed for weapon fire. A high-pitched hiss tells you even before the console alarm does: The hull is punctured and you're depressurizing! There are certainly emergency suits somewhere aboard, but you can't get at them while Jorth is on your tail.

The eternal cold of space seeps in as the pressure drops. Gash can handle the lower pressure for a while, but you haven't got a thick, scaly hide. You gasp for breath, your chest hurts, and your vision grows hazy.

"You cannot escape, Hayl!" Jorth cackles.

A completely unnecessary remark, you think bitterly. Domain governors have no style at all.

Nothing for it but to dive back down into the atmosphere of Pellaj, hoping to lose him in clouds.

Pushing down on the controls, you begin the dive, with Jorth's yacht close enough behind to read your registry numbers.

As you screech back into air, the yacht clings to your vapor-trail. Gash barks in alarm as the hull heats up; your shields were damaged, and now the temperature is rising by the moment. But bailing out would be insane, even if it were possible.

You're hit again! The stabilizers may go at any moment, so you have to level out. Last thing I wanted to do, you tell yourself. Maybe it's the last thing I will do.

The freighter's hull screams with strain as you pull back on the throttle. But the stabilizers hold, and you bottom out just above the waters of Pellaj. Down from the clouds zooms Jorth's ship. He must have you square in his sights. "Well, it's been fun," you say.

Then you look again at those clouds. One of them is floating down after Jorth's ship—a shiny white cloud—no, a ship! An airship, larger than a Morione heavy cruiser, the largest vehicle you've ever seen!

From the freighter's radio come bizarre moaning sounds—words of the Cetapod language. "It's theirs!" you shout to Gash. "It's a ship built for Cetapods!"

The tremendous ship looms overhead. The air hums with vibrations from its powerful antigravs. Jorth must have finally noticed it because the yacht breaks away with a snap-roll and heads for open air. But a dozen bright rays from the airship lance out with unerring accuracy. The explosion hurts your eyes, but you don't mind this particular pain. "*Hrrrraaaarrrgh!*" cries Gash, paraphrasing a traditional G'rax victory cry.

Debris rains down around you as you and Gash cheer. Another victory for the Resistance! And, just as important, you actually survived.

The Cetapod ship pulls your ailing freighter into a docking bay. The tiny spacecraft is dwarfed by the atmospheric ship, the way a man would be dwarfed by—well, a Cetapod. As a courtesy, the owners have removed the water from your bay.

Not long after, you're floating in an atmo-bubble on the bridge of the airship. Through the clear plastoid wall and the water beyond, you look down on a dozen Cetapods as they pilot the gigantic ship. Their tentacles manipulate throttle sticks as tall as trees and twist knobs that would make huge dinner tables. The control consoles look as big as your ship.

With you is Tandon Rey, commander of the human Resistance on Pellaj. "This ship, the *Ssaurahauuula*, uh—well, we'd call it the *Vengeance*—has been under construction since Jorth took over here. They just got it airborne today."

"Nice timing."

"The Cetapods were going to launch an attack on the *Ocean Lord* as soon as their leader escaped. They didn't expect to survive. Good to see the sacrifice wasn't needed—and we did manage to take care of Jorth after all, as it turned out."

"Yeah. Nice timing. Did I say that?"

"Jorth is gone, the stronghold is gone, and the *Vengeance* is airworthy," says Tandon Rey. "Now it looks like the Cetapods can protect Pellaj from the Domain."

"Good thing they're on our side. If this thing could make it into space, I don't know what would protect anybody from the Cetapods."

It's time to leave Pellaj.

If you have already been to the Dvaad asteroid mine in this adventure, go to 93.

If you have not yet gone to Dvaad, go to 25.

4

You have to get away from the stronghold quickly. Only two ships look ready for liftoff.

Will you choose the beautiful, powerful starcruiser yacht, too posh to be anything but Baron Jorth's private ship?

Or will you instead take the inconspicuous old freighter—not glamorous, but sturdy?

If you choose Baron Jorth's private yacht, go to 71.
If you choose the sturdy freighter, go to 3.

5

The tracking device shows you a simple directional arrow leading toward the Cetapod's homing locator. Another readout shows distance—quite a walk ahead.

Through winding corridors, skylit halls, and a maze of offices you track the signal. You can't risk checking the locator too often, because the stronghold is infested with Domain soldiers and security cameras. A fortress!

In a hallway near the core of the city, you risk another look at the indicator. Good, the signal is close by. But so is a shadow that falls across the device. You look up—right into the muzzle of a Domain blaster rifle. "You're caught, Hayl," says the soldier.

The guard leads you down a hallway to a high-security door labeled GOVERNOR'S OFFICE. It slides back, and you enter a luxuriously furnished room. On a low table of polished grellwood, you see the Resistance homing device.

Go to 88.

6

"Our headquarters was about to be raided," says
the local Resistance commander, Tandon Rey. "So
Tharrahaussal, our hostess here, offered us the perfect replacement HQ: herself."

His voice echoes from the creature's rib cage. Resistance planning tables and command screens float on
rubber rafts in dilute digestive fluid. Bright lamps
hover just beneath the spine. Skimmers and supplies
rest on moist, fleshy organs. The damp air blows in
two directions as the Cetapod breathes, carrying a
rank, wet smell. "Nice decor," you observe.

Tandon takes a swallow from a squeezebulb full of
singflower tea. He's a tall, skeletal, half-bearded
human from one of the asteroid habitats in the Kanta
system. "You take what you can get when you're
fighting Jorth. That slimy, fat gravel-maggot has been
feeding on the body of Pellaj for too long. He's hunt-
ing the Cetapods and torturing their leader. He
started the mining operation that's spoiling the
ocean. He supervises the 'fishing trips.' You know
about those? They harvest sea life, 'accidentally'
including Cetapods, and render them down into food
and oil."

"But the Cetapods are sentient!"

"Yes, intelligent beings, Hayl, as smart and individual as you or I, being turned into circuit cleaner
and narcotic incense and salted caviar for expensive
parties. Baron Jorth's work."

"What a lowdown, swill-eating, Domain-level—"
you run out of adjectives to describe Baron Jorth.
"Who is the Cetapod leader that Jorth is torturing?"

"Haurrassith is ruler of the Cetapods, and a strong
supporter of the Resistance. The Domains caught him
when he tried to place a melter-net underneath the
Ocean Lord, Jorth's stronghold. Now Jorth is holding

him there in a torture tank. No one knows how much longer Haurrassith will hold up."

"You must have tried breaking him out," you say.

"Of course. But security is tight, and we're not sure where they're holding him. We can't attack in force—large commando groups stand out like a berserker at a cocktail party. We've tried single operatives."

"Any luck?"

"They haven't returned. We can't risk any more forces right now. You're headed in there anyway, on this suicidal rescue mission. If you have the opportunity. . . ."

"Right."

After talking with Tandon, you follow him to a floating table. It rides low in the digestive juices under the weight of equipment, some rather bulky. "As long as you're throwing yourself into Jorth's hands on this mission," says Tandon, "we might as well help as much as we can. This is what passes for our arsenal and equipment section, since the evacuation. Take your pick."

Blasters, stun guns, gas projectors, nothing much of interest. "What's this bit of junk?" you ask, lifting a handheld unit with a broken readout screen.

"That *was* a homing device," Tandon says. "Tracks down signals from locating beacons that our agents swallow. We were going to use it to find Haurrassith, the imprisoned Cetapod leader, but it got shot up in our last raid."

"What's that? Broken machinery?" Wrench asks. "Say, why don't I have a look at that? After all, fixing things is my job. Also cleaning up," Wrench continues, stripping down the tracking device and bending a few automatic arms over it. "Though I'm lost as to where to start in this place. Oh, Commander, I should mention for your safety that such an environment can produce many diseases in humans, especially the crawling-fungus sickness, which is invariably fatal. Good luck!" The bot hums happily over his work.

Tandon looks a bit gray. "Is that a Domain demoralization robot?" he asks you.

"No. But he does seem willing to think about the unthinkable. At every opportunity."

In a matter of minutes Wrench has repaired the small tracking device. You think it might be useful because Gash may be with the captive Cetapod. The Domain often groups nonhumans together on a base so they don't disrupt the nice orderly lines of soldiers. So if you find the Cetapod, you find Gash. Maybe.

You take the tracking device, then indicate a couple of harness devices on the table. "What are those two things?"

"This first one is a miniaturized antigrav unit designed just for espionage work," Tandon explains. "You can float long enough to plant a bomb on a wall or fly over a surveillance net. Somewhat impractical for everyday use because its power supply lasts only a few uses, and the shielding isn't much good."

"Great," you mutter, strapping it on. It's kind of heavy, but you decide it could help you on your mission. "And this other thing?"

The second item is a computer and speaker, a Cetapod translation device. It's a small box that clips onto your harness, with a chest-mounted speaker grille. "Think of it as a translator bot in a box," says Tandon.

"Sounds horrible," you say.

"This one has no personality."

"Sounds better already."

Tandon tells you more. When you activate the device and speak into a throat-mike, the robot processor translates your words into Cetapod speech. "Cover your ears when it's on," warns Tandon.

"Cetapod talk is deafening." Likewise, the device will take a Cetapod's words and relay them to you in your own language, through an ear receiver.

After the Resistance technicians outfit you with all this equipment, you and Wrench prepare to leave the Resistance base. Tandon pleads for you to rethink your mission. "Hayl, you're too smart to waste—"

"How many times am I supposed to give the same speech?" you say angrily. "Everyone is telling me to desert Zygash. Everyone should stop. Now." Tandon shuts up.

The Resistance fighters tell you what they know of the *Ocean Lord* floating stronghold. It's so big and so well defended you haven't much chance of even finding Gash, let alone getting out alive with him.

"When do I leave?" you question, trying to cover up your uneasiness.

You and a team of swimmers put on breather masks and head underwater for the citadel. Tandon's own sea-skimmer leads the way. The vehicle's sleek nose and streamlined pontoons easily cut through the water. Tagging on the back of the skimmer, you see Tandon trigger the counter-electronics that foil the Domain defense systems. Soon you're skimming beneath a metal-and-concrete expanse that fills your vision, like an upside-down spaceport.

Swimming away from the skimmer, you reach a recessed hatchway with a force field that creates a globe of air. At the hatch a Resistance infiltrator pulls you aboard. Like a germ infecting a huge monster, you penetrate the underbelly of the *Ocean Lord*.

Go to 21.

7

In deep space, far from any help, you must rely on your own strength to pull yourself over the hull of the *Small Waist*. Hand over hand you crawl across its belly, narrowly avoiding the gravity generators. Up the ridged entry shield you go, until you reach the sensor suite holding the vital navigational arrays.

Through the hull you feel the vibrations of the eDrive system as it warms up for a jump. Fear stabs at you, and maybe this fear gives you the strength to break the navigational dishes. But your leverage is wrong, and the effort sends you falling across the face of the ship, directly in front of the main viewport.

Inside, Jaspon is naturally startled. "Hayl!" he cries over the radio. "You're blocking my view. I can't see where we're going!"

"I can, Jaspon, and believe me, you don't want to."

Without navigation sensors, the *Small Waist* blunders right into the fabric statue hanging in front of it. Shirts rip and wires tangle in the external fixtures. In a moment, starting with the left hip and quickly pulling in the rest of the body, the entire statue collapses around you. The ship rips through, sending shreds of white fabric swirling into the void. Another sad story in the annals of sculpture.

You hear the miner's sobs. "This is your doing, Hayl. All that effort, I just want to—but no, you will not crush me! I shall rebuild anew. I shall add your shredded lifesuit to the fabric of my masterwork, and your body I shall consign to the infinite deep!"

"Oh, you shall, shall you?" Still chilly with fear, you search for another tactic. Break into the ship through a weak point? Unfortunately, the only weak point you can think of in this mining vessel calls for you to crawl directly up the rear thruster port. Oh, well.

You know the thruster port will soon grow too hot

to enter. You scrabble as fast as you can across the topside hull of the *Small Waist*, over the rear heat-guards.

The port glows red-hot as you arrive. The lifesuit protects you from the heat—so why is sweat dripping in your eyes? You flounder, weightless, looking for the protected circuit panel. There! As the thruster glows brighter, you rip open the panel and, with one punch, short the circuits inside. Not a moment to spare!

Now the ship cannot move or jump into eDrive. You cross the circuits, make one thruster coil glow blue-hot, and burn a hole through the bulkhead. With a gust of air, the cabin depressurizes, almost blowing you out of the port and into infinite darkness. But you hold on, and soon Jaspon himself blows against the hole and stops the flow of air.

Gasping for air, Jaspon puts up little fight. You fit

him with a breathing mask, seal the breach with fast-congealing hullfoam, and replace the shorted circuits with standard substitutes from the repair compartment. Piece of cake!

You don't know where in space you are, but luckily Jaspon has already plotted his course. You find it appropriate to tie up Jaspon with his own shirt. Then you settle in for the trip.

Jaspon soon falls into exhausted sleep, and he snores loudly. Not only that, he talks in his sleep. "Gzzzaw. Gzznt! Gzz . . . oh, 'f course, Director, I know 'is is secure area—gzzz—no, no! I'm auth'rized t' visit Dvaad, got to apply for work there. Password 'fusion furnace,' tol' me so yourself—gzzzaw . . ."

If you can believe Jaspon's mumbling, this is the current Domain password! It makes sense that Jaspon would have to know it to obtain entrance to a Domain mine. "Director" is probably a personnel director, responsible for finding job candidates willing to tolerate the Domain's low wages and bad working conditions. You make a mental note of that password: "fusion furnace."

Jaspon doesn't wake up until you've dropped out of eDrive in the Dalorvan Minor system. You push his bed out the airlock into the waiting miner's aid station. There the meditechs will turn him into a normal person, if possible. With his ship, the *Small Waist*, you continue to the asteroid mine called Dvaad. Then you're ready to face the Domain.

Go to 58.

8

Using a net and dagger against a G'rax with a blaster, your chance of success matches that of—how would you put it?—a snowball in a fusion reactor. So you spring to battle with a fairly clear conscience, even though you're fighting your best friend. After all, if you can't possibly hurt him, why worry?

First, you have to get rid of that blaster. Last time you sparred with Gash, at the Resistance base on Silverlight a few standard days ago, he still hadn't licked that habit of shying away reflexively from a sudden sharp movement by his right eye. He developed that after a childhood encounter with a Carelaxian poisonfly, and he still has it.

You throw the weighted net at just the right spot— yep! Gash flinches. In that split-second you jump in and bring the dagger in a shallow slicing cut across his lower right forearm. The blade bounces off his scales, but the blaster drops. Catching it, you heave it far away, out of the fight.

Then Gash heaves *you* far away, with a painful kick that, even before you land, feels like it popped a couple of ribs. Ignoring the pain (if an understated "Aaargh!" counts as ignoring it), you wait for him to lumber toward you. Not yet—not yet—now! You swing the net to tangle his feet, then pull. Gash falls hard, and you beat him back up. Running, you pull the net over him, trapping him.

Before you realize what you're doing, you stab with the dagger. When his scales turn dark green with blood, you see he's badly hurt. What a sight. And you came here to rescue him!

"Hayl!" Jorth shouts, furious that his "show" had an unexpected climax. "Don't kill him, or Carabajal will make you regret it!" So Duke Carabajal ordered you and Gash kept alive. Why? You have no time to wonder. The troopers jeer your cowardice, urging you to kill Zygash. Seeing the G'rax lying at your feet, you know you can't hurt him again, even if it means he kills you instead.

Gash looks at you with a new expression—no, an old expression. "*Hrrrnnhhgh*," he growls weakly. Startled, you bend closer. Sure enough, the shock of injury has snapped him out of the mind control!

"Play along with me, Gash," you whisper. "I think the good guys are going to win this one, after all."

Go to 14.

9

The ship controls! You leap for the throttle and twist, holding tight to the acceleration straps with your free hand. The ship yaws sharply. Gash and Jorth both fall to the deck before the inertial dampers can cut in.

Zygash is on the governor in an instant, grabbing the blaster and pulling back two fists for a double roundhouse punch. But with inhuman speed Jorth's pudgy arm shoots up and catches Gash under the chin. The purple head snaps back, and the gigantic G'rax slips to the deck. Zygash, stunned with a punch!

A bolt of energy strikes your hand as you pull back on the throttle. You cry out in pain. "Do not consider that again, Hayl!" says Jorth shrilly.

Nursing your wounded hand, you can only wonder how this puny governor got to be such a good shot. It's those bulges at his arm-joints; you could swear you heard something whirring.

Jorth orders you away from the controls, and he really means it. You know that he just wants you to move to the center of the cabin, away from the viewport. That way he can shoot you in cold blood without endangering the ship. But what can you do?

Gash must realize the same thing, because he

growls his fiercest growl. Such language! Jorth bridles at the insults. "You have caused enough trouble as well, creature," he hisses. He raises the blaster to point directly at Zygash's forehead.

That gives you the chance to jump him. You knock his arm, the shot goes wild, and down you both go into a heap. You have no time to wonder whether the shot punctured the hull because you're in a fight with Baron Jorth himself!

Go to 28.

10

The rest of your trip proceeds uneventfully. You sigh with relief to see the waterworld of Pellaj hanging in space ahead. It's a pure blue globe dusted with white clouds. With no trace of land, from orbit it seems a serene place. But the serenity is an illusion, for the Domain has plunged Pellaj into slavery.

Its waters contain, in dissolved form, the minerals that make the galaxy run: rare earths, zirconium, and superheavies. The scion governor on Pellaj, Baron Jorth of Clan Carabajal, has enslaved the native race, the Cetapods, to obtain this wealth. From his floating stronghold, the only Domain base on the planet, he rules with cruelty unusual even for the Domain.

The Cetapods are unique in all the galaxy. Huge beyond comprehension, some as big as space-cruisers, they swim in the blue-green seas, for only the water can support their weight. You've seen holos of the Cetapods, with their rounded, streamlined contours, powerful tails, and the twin clumps of manipulating tentacles high on their heads. Hard to believe it, but these creatures are highly intelligent.

If you got here on the Resistance ship *Rustbucket*, go to 55.

If you arrived on a Worldways commercial spaceliner, go to 70.

If you took another ship, go to 89.

11

Wrench scurries to patch through a repair program. With pincers sealing duct leaks, and with who knows what electronic jiggery-pokery, Wrench convinces the *Rustbucket* that it's really in fair working order. The stabilizer quits acting up and the life-support unit decides you should live.

Now all you have to worry about is the jump to eDrive. With the star's surface rushing by beneath you, the timing for the jump will be crucial. If you're too close to the star when you hit the jump-button, you'll probably explode (or, at very least, be thrown far off course). If you're too far away, the sun's gravity will pull you back, slowing you down too much for the old inertial eDrive to work.

You watch the chronometer, trying to think of nothing at all.

But now the coronals have noticed you. They scamper playfully alongside your ship as you build up velocity, for they can move at almost light speed without effort. As the plasma-beings loop and roll, distracting you, the *Rustbucket* plunges toward the sun.

The light beneath you is too bright, painfully bright. Prominences flare on either side, and you sail beneath the glowing arch of a stellar flare big enough to circle the largest planet in the galaxy. You can see it all through your closed eyelids.

In a breath, you're away from the star. But its gravity, which sped you into eDrive, now tries to hold you back. The old ship creaks and strains. This calls for great skill and timing: You must wait until you're far enough away from the star to enter eDrive safely, but if you wait too long you'll be moving too slowly to reach eDrive.

You hit the control, launch into eDrive, breathe a relieved sigh, and suddenly you're tossed on your head. The *Rustbucket* flips unexpectedly back to normal drive and begins to break up.

Every control goes dead and the cabin goes dark. You look out at the stars and see nothing at all familiar. Where are you? You look out the other viewport—and just stare.

Out there, hanging in empty space, is a gigantic white statue. It's apparently a human being, with features you can't make out; you're drifting down by the boots. On close inspection, you see it's actually a wire frame, and stretched between its struts are pieces of fabric. The fabric is weird and oddly shaped, like— clothing? Are those *shirts*?

"Ho there!" comes a voice. The emergency radio has blinked on with an incoming signal. "Enjoying my work, are you? I'm deeply gratified to see an art-lover coming to view my humble labor."

You leap for the radio. "Mayday, mayday, emergency, I need rescue here! Can you home in on my signal?"

"My dear chap, I can see you from here. No need to get worked up, I'll be with you momentarily."

In a short while, a simple mining ship zooms in and links up with you, airlock to airlock. You and Wrench cross over into the *Small Waist*. You enter a tight cabin with an open cockpit, one sleeping berth, and a pilot who introduces himself as Jaspon Dentoze. You recall that name from the ship registry on

Silverlight—the miner who wanted company on a trip to Dvaad. Looks like he didn't get it.

Jaspon says, "This surprising opportunity for companionship is most pleasant. For years I have wanted to show off my masterwork to an appreciative viewer."

"Are those—um—shirts?"

"Yes, indeed. I was once a shirt designer. After I finally escaped that dismal trade, I found a brilliant new use for all those old shirts. For the moment I am paying bills as a miner, but soon I expect to become renowned as an artist throughout the galaxy. And you—you said your name is Hayl?—you, Hayl, have the privilege of seeing it first."

The statue, of course, is a self-portrait. From his small craft you see the whole thing in its (for lack of a better word) glory. "What's that on its nose?" you ask.

"Aack!" says Dentoze. "A vile insult, that's what it is! A meteoroid or somesuch has swept away the fabric on the tip of the frame. You—Hayl, your name is?—Hayl, give me your shirt, so that I may repair the injury."

"Say what?"

"Come, come, is it that hard a request? Give me your shirt! Why do you hesitate?"

"Things have been moving kind of fast recently, Jaspon. Let me think."

Go to 46.

12

The spaceliner's casino is an extravaganza of purple velvet, silver chandeliers, noisy tourists, and games of all kinds: hologram boards, jubilee wheels, card games like liar's cut and catch hyper, disk machines, and high sky dice tables. Most of the patrons look about one million times wealthier than you, but gambling is gambling. You're in your element.

You sit at a hyper table and buy in for a small stake. As you play, you strike up a conversation with a lady on the next stool. She's a fairly old, fairly fat human with maybe a touch of Wyzean blood, dressed in a shapeless shimmersilk gown. Her eyebrows are jewelled, her nostrils pierced, and she positively oozes wealth.

"Chasma Hoyd," she says, introducing herself. "I lead the Planetary Committee to—oh, goody, I've won again, hahaha! Where was I? Oh, yes, the committee to declare the floating gaspbladder the official Pellajian plant. Have you heard of our movement? Oh, well, we shall be better known by and by."

It's slightly staggering to realize that for this woman the Domain and the Resistance simply don't exist. Her world is comfortable and isolated. Takes all kinds to make a galaxy, you suppose. You push forward another wager.

A commotion begins behind you. You turn, but a public announcement calms you. "This is the captain. We've happened on a flock of Ilirishi, folks. Nothing to worry about, but try to stay clear of them as they pass through."

You see one of the Ilirishi now, a quivering white blob passing through a card table. It changes shape several times as you watch. "Whuh—what is it?" asks Chasma Hoyd. Her eyes are bulging, her winnings forgotten.

"Four-dimensional creatures that live in eSpace," you explain. "Not much is known about them. All we see is their three-dimensional cross section, as they pass through the ship." You can't help thinking of these floating, wobbling, ever-changing blobs as inquisitive tourists. Like tourists, they will eventually move on, shrinking and vanishing into eSpace.

You sit back to watch the unscheduled show, but Chasma squeals in panic. "It's floating this way, it's—this way, I—"

"My lady," you tell Chasma Hoyd, "believe me, it's just a curious animal. I've seen them twice myself and nothing happened, except things got knocked around a little. Calm down. . . ."

It's not working. The dowager's cheeks are puffing and her pierced nostrils are flaring like slathorp suckers.

If you try again to talk sense into Chasma Hoyd, go to 22.

If you decide to slap her to wake her from this frenzy, go to 61.

If you just let her run around, go to 64.

13

The Hotjets bar looks none too hot these days. Its main dome is cracked, the climate controls are shot (literally), and blaster scorches on the walls tell of many differences of opinion. In the dark, muggy atmosphere of the tavern, Kregg the alien informant fits right in.

First you find the bartender, a blue, scaly Vhurrg. She's seen some history; you can tell by her scars. With eye patches covering two of her sockets, she has just three beady eyes left to stare you down. "Stella!" you cry jovially. "It's me, Rogan Hayl, remember?"

"*Za hagoosh. Horba za di-hoggabrol valorgh vo-trees-blood, Hayl.*"

"What a memory!" you say, suppressing a shiver. "Whoops, there's my old buddy Kregg. I'll be right back to settle up on that debt, don't you worry. Oh, and get me a flask of treesblood, thanks." With the music of Zook Batly's Throbbing Throm Band in the

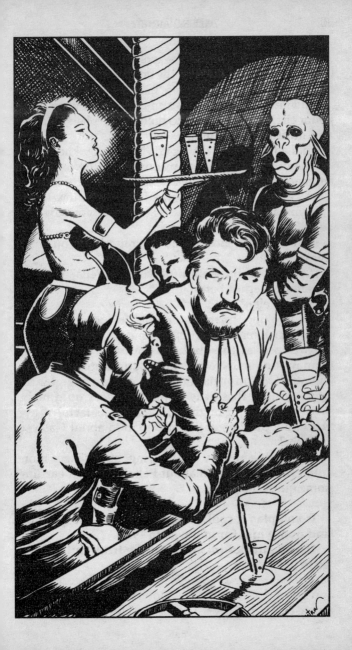

background, you walk toward the shapeless figure perched on a high stool at the end of the bar.

"Hello, Hayl," says Kregg, his wrinkled face almost hidden in the folds of his sun-coat. "You want ztuff 'bout the G'rax, right?" He holds a purplish drink in one gray, fingerless hand.

"News travels fast, Kregg. What do you know?"

"Had call from acquaintanze of mine on board Domain's docking ztation. Reziztanze fighter Zygash G'rax arrivez there, big newz. Pay cloze attenzion to his deztinazion, you know." He watches you sidelong with large, sad-looking eyes.

You pass him most of the debit markers you have. "Talk."

"Zygash visiting beautiful world of Pellaj, home of revered governor Baron Jorth."

"Why Pellaj?"

"No nozion. Jorth making bid for power, zo they zay. Zygash maybe part of zcheme."

You look at the slicktop counter, where your money still lies. Kregg is being uncommonly generous with his information. He keeps darting glances at you out of that little wrinkled face. Could he be worried that you might not believe his facts? Why? And how did he get the information about Gash so quickly?

You decide he may not be lying, but he's got more interest in telling you about Pellaj than just earning some quick money.

If you play it cool, pretend you're not suspicious, and pump him for more, go to 19.

If you attack him and beat the truth out of him, go to 24.

14

You and Gash both stand near the balcony, as though ready to continue the battle. Above you, Jorth and the soldiers are cheering, hungry for blood. Gash raises his rifle to point at you—

—Then he pulls it up to point at the arena rails, and fires a long burst that sends the soldiers diving for cover!

"Waaaa-hoooo!" you shout, throwing the net. One end snags Jorth. It traps him in his bodychair and keeps him from pushing a button to escape.

"*Vrrraaaanggghaagh!*"

"If you can climb faster, *you* do it!" You struggle up the net. Now the soldiers rush back to the railing and fire at both of you. In the barrage of bolts, you reach the balcony and vault the railing. Then, with one motion, you pull Jorth's blaster from his holster and aim it at his temple. "Say it," you tell him.

Jorth's eyes bulge, and his tongue sticks out between pudgy lips. "Ho-ho-hold your fire!" he squeals. The troopers stop their barrage, and soon Gash climbs out of the arena pit to join you.

"Well handled, Captain Hayl!" says Wrench as he wheels over to join you.

"What about a trip to the launching area?" you ask cheerfully.

Go to 85.

15

You walk across the spaceport tarmac toward the distant maintenance complex. That building, low and inconspicuous beneath the silvery clouds of the planet Silverlight, could hardly hold off the Domain forces that would descend on it—*if* the Domain knew it held a Resistance base.

The sky is radiant with diffuse light, and the wind has the tang of Silverlight's far-off forests. But the spaceport looks just like the hundreds you've seen in your wanderings across the Galaxy. You visit so many worlds.

At the nearest entrance to the maintenance building you're stopped by a thin, angular guard robot. "Password, sir?" it asks.

You forgot to get the password from Owen. Well, no problem. The Resistance hasn't shown much originality in passwords. "Oh, let's see," you tell the robot, "I knew it up to the moment you asked me. No, don't tell me! Umm . . . 'Freedom'?"

"No, sir."

"No, right, that's an old one, isn't it? Wait, wait, I've got it, 'Liberation'!"

"No, sir, that was the last one."

"Right, how silly of me. 'Tyranny falls'?"

"Oh, that's a good one!" says the robot. "We haven't used that one yet."

"Yeah, I like it. . . . 'Independence'?"

"Yes, sir. Go right in."

Robots can be so dumb, you think as you enter a shadowed corridor. The walkway leads to a high-roofed hangar crowded with equipment, lifting machines, dismantled ships, and Resistance fighters. One, a short, stocky woman whose blond hair sweeps down across her forehead, wears the insignia of a Resistance commander.

She finishes giving an order, turns, and sees you. At once her blaster is in her hand, pointed right at you. "Hayl!" she shouts, and a hundred other blasters follow hers.

Reflexively your hand hits your holster, but it would be stupid to draw here. "Relax," you say.

"What do you think, that I've joined the Domain?"

No one has lowered a weapon yet. "Your scaly co-pilot did, so we figure you have too," says the commander, Jorah.

"Gash hasn't joined anything, except the Resistance! You're all as easy to fool as that passbot. Please, put down your weapons and tell me how to find my friend."

Eventually you convince them. Jorah tells you what she knows: "Our spy aboard the docking station says the *Genesis* was taken to Dvaad, an asteroid mine in the Dalorvan Minor system. But the G'rax didn't go with it."

"He went to Pellaj. Old news." You've never heard of Dvaad before today. "What do they want with my ship at an asteroid mine?"

"The spy says there're tech labs there. The Domain wants to tear down your ship to see what makes it move."

"Ouch. Look, I need a ship—bad. What can you give me?"

The answer turns out to be "not much." Zygash destroyed most of the available Resistance ships when he left. The only one that's spaceworthy right now is an obsolete rimrunner courier with tin seats and no food synthesizer. It's not promising, but you make a note of the Resistance ship's hangar number anyway.

"What's it called?" you ask.

"Originally, the *Snapdragon Wine*, I think," says Jorah. "We renamed it *Rustbucket*."

"Great."

If you're ready to leave Silverlight in this monstrosity now, go to 40.

If you visit Kregg the stoolie, go to 29.

To leave Silverlight in some other way, go to 45.

16

You decide to get some rest after your adventures. In your luxurious cabin, you get one of the most restful sleeps you've had since you joined the Resistance.

Still, you wake up in poor spirits, for you miss Zygash. You think of the G'rax's rough humor, his fierce loyalty and courage, and the great times you've had together. How could anyone believe he's joined the Domain?

The ceiling speaker in your cabin buzzes. "We've got a few new passengers all of a sudden, folks," says the captain's voice. "A flock of Ilirishi has gotten curious about us. They may knock over a few dishes in the officers' mess, or push your beds around a little, but they're completely harmless. Just ignore them, and they'll go away."

Ignore an Ilirishi! You grin at the idea of ignoring a four-dimensional eSpace creature that changes shape and size from moment to moment. You've encountered them twice on the *Genesis*, and both times were wonder-shows like you never imagined. Good thing they're not hostile, because they can appear at random in any room on a ship.

—Like this one! Here in your stateroom, a blobby white sphere shivers into view, then grows before your eyes. Odd veins surface and vanish on its leathery skin—if it is skin, and not a crosssection of some fourth-dimension internal organ.

Your human eyes see only a moving, three-dimensional "cutaway view" of the creature as it passes through your cabin. You try to picture what the thing looks like with all these three-dimensional shapes strung together in a higher reality, then give up the attempt.

Suddenly the Ilirishi grows a bulbous many-colored patch that may be an eye. It must be, for it sees you and moves toward you!

You could roll off the bed, out of the creature's way, and it would seep through the wall and vanish. Or you could let it absorb you just to see what happens; you've done crazier things in your stellar career.

If you evade the creature, go to 10.
If you *want* to be absorbed, go to 66.

17

With the sounds of mining machinery thrumming along the tunnels like a heartbeat, you can almost imagine Dvaad to be a living organism. In this part of the complex the tunnels have been drilled straight and clean. Technicians in lab uniforms carry exotic scientific equipment, and the robots are made for technical work. You walk unnoticed among them.

Every so often the asteroid's natives, the white insect-things, aimlessly crawl by. Everyone ignores them. The little things look as lost as you are. You wonder how you're going to find anything, let alone your ship, in this labyrinth. You could walk across the galaxy before you located anything the Domain wants to hide. After all, your ship is obviously a valuable prize, probably guarded with highest security, scrutinized with laborious care. . . .

You turn a corner into an open hangar, and there's the *Prosperogenesis*.

No one's around; the door stands wide open. Joy, anger, and embarrassment all rise in you. Then all give way to pain, when you see that maintenance robots and loaderbots are tearing your ship apart!

The gangway lies dismantled, circuitry and pipes sprawl everywhere, both blaster pods have been removed, and even the cockpit seats are gone. In a

neglected corner lies Zygash's treesblood distiller,
and for some reason that's the sight that drives home
the whole horrible idea. The Domain is disassem-
bling your ship to see what makes it go.

Fighting back tears, you stumble toward the hulk
of your beloved freighter. Oh—oh, no! It breaks your
heart to see the *Genesis's* internals scattered around.
Every panel hangs open; all the circuits have been
gutted. You notice they haven't yet found your smuggling caches, down under the floorboards, but it's
only a matter of time.

In the cockpit you stare out through windowless
viewports. Robots haul away parts of your ship to
designated spots on the hangar floor. Staring out at
that array, you think they might as well have dismembered you instead. Over there, instead of cables,
would be your nerves and tendons; across the room,
where the gravitic supports lie, your bones would
slowly bleach in the hangar's fluorescent light. Looking at it all, you give way to sweet self-pity.

You think, That's my whole ship out there. After a
moment the rest of that thought hits hard:

It's all still there!

Burning with hope, you look with experienced
eyes across the hangar. You've taken the *Genesis* apart
often enough. You can see that, if it's not all here, then
at least most of its parts are still in this room.

You grab a portable data display lying on the dismantled console. On its screen you find a shipyard
manifest, a list showing the disposition of the *Genesis's*
many parts. Scrolling down its lengthy list, you see that
only two essential systems have been removed from
the hangar. Techs took the power cores to a nearby storage room (standard procedure with volatile items), and
the eDrive system has gone to this area's Tech Lab for
study. The *Genesis* can't get off the ground without both
of these—but now you know where they are.

Why waste time? "Wrench, put this ship back together."

"Aye, sir," says the bot. It shouts at another Merpie beneath the cockpit port. "New orders. Get your crew to start putting this ship back together, pronto!"

"On what authority?" asks the robot uncertainly.

You pick out the authorization number from the top of the factboard and give it to the robot. Without further comment, the bot picks up a piece of equipment and carries it back on board. Across the hangar, all the other robots (clearly linked by radio to the first one) stop and reverse their tracks, carrying the parts aboard. Wrench, busily supervising them, seems to forget you're here.

Good enough. Now you have to fetch the other two systems before a human discovers the new, fictitious, orders. First, you need to get to the power cores. You call up a map on the factboard, then use it to guide you down a short tunnel to a door of molded metal. Marked STORAGE, it looks quite thick. Hmmm.

You see guards, technicians, and more of those white many-legged natives. No one in this tunnel looks like a good choice to let you into the room.

A maintenance robot rolls by, and you decide it's the lowest-risk opportunity. "Hey, robot, I've lost my keycode to this area. Let me in here, will you?"

"Sorry, sir," it squeaks, "but I can't let you in unless you have proper authorization."

You slump against the tunnel wall. "Oh, no," you moan, "then I guess that poor robot is doomed."

"I beg your pardon, sir?"

"No, don't be sorry, you're only doing your job. I'm sure that poor, damaged bot would forgive you, even though the lubricant it needs after that railgun accident is just an arm's length away." You shed a tear.

"Is the damage great, sir?"

"Oh, don't worry about it." You keep your voice

level, as though heroically suppressing grief. "You have your duty to do, just as it tried to do its own. It's going to destabilize before I can get that clearance, but I'm sure it would be comforted to know that a fellow robot did its duty—"

"My apologies, sir," says the robot. Even a mechanical can sound contrite, you discover. "Please give the unit my best wishes for a speedy repair." It keys in a code, then hurries on as the door opens.

The storage room is close and dimly lit, smelling of a hundred scents from engine lubricant to incense. Shelves crammed full of supplies rise to a high ceiling. Sidling down the aisles, you think of the prices these goods could fetch on the smuggling runs you've made. Look there—gondwana juice! And beside it, a frigicask of Polarian ale. Must be for the officers' mess, you decide.

Then you spot the power cores from the *Prospero-*

genesis. They're so big that you can't carry away anything else from here, more's the pity. But you'll have a tavern tale about the big haul that got away, if you get through this alive.

You lug the power cores to the door, then enlist a passing robot to carry them down the tunnel to the *Genesis*'s hangar. For once you're not much worried that you'll be discovered. You learned long ago that a thief could walk out of a palace with the Fire Jewels of Kierka if he just looks like he belongs there.

Once you've dropped off the power cores inside the dismantled ship, you go for the eDrive system. Following the factboard map, you come to an open hatchway farther down the tunnel. It's labeled TECHNICAL LABORATORY. Sure enough, through it you can see lots of scientific equipment and machinery of all kinds. Everything from mining drills to robot integrators lies everywhere, in various stages of repair. Nobody's home; they must be out on a break.

Nothing too interesting . . . but what pulls you in the door is the sight of the *Prosperogenesis*'s own eDrive system. It sits on a lab table, whole, ready to be dismantled. Well, you'll see about that!

You hear voices behind you—the lab's technicians are returning.

If you hide from the technicians, go to 34.

If you confront them and try to bluff them, go to 78.

If you pull your blaster and attack them, go to 75.

18

The huge chamber is lined with machinery and gantryways. White panels near the high ceiling provide pale light, but tanks of liquid and masses of

crates and barrels make the room a gloomy place.
You hear the hum of machines, the rumbling moan of
a Cetapod, and the growl of a G'rax.

The largest thing in the room is a giant torture tank
filled with bubbling clear fluid. The largest thing in
the tank, and probably on the planet, is Haurrassith,
the Cetapod that leads the Resistance on Pellaj. The
creature's huge, streamlined body stretches longer
than a dozen copies of the *Prosperogenesis* laid end to
end. At the head, above a strangely human-looking
eye, you see two clusters of bright red manipulator
tentacles, shivering with pain.

Next to the Cetapod's torture tank is a much
smaller one. Suspended in the tank is Zygash the
G'rax. His four arms float at odd angles to his huge
purple body, and bubbles rise around him. His mouth
is open in agony, revealing many sharp teeth. His
moans carry through the tank fluid.

Two soldiers with blaster rifles stand between the
Cetapod's tank and Gash's. You hear talk of new models of sea-skimmers, jibes about officers and drill
sergeants, and at last the conversation turns to the prisoners. "Thought this G'rax was on our side," says one.

"He was. Then he went traitor a while back, and
Jorth popped him in here."

You see nothing to do but attack the guards. But
maybe Gash can help you with a diversion.

You hide behind a bank of calibration equipment
near Gash's tank, then wait until both guards happen
to be looking in another direction. Then you signal to
Gash in the torture tank. He sees your wave and
howls in surprise. But the guards take it as just
another moan of pain.

Gash is smart enough to figure out that you need a
diversion. He begins pounding on the tank walls,
roaring for rescue, and pointing—not at you, but in
the opposite direction. "Shut up, you!" say the

guards, distracted. Raising their rifles, they go to investigate the supposed "rescuer." You sneak over to the torture tank.

You gesture to Zygash to squeeze over to one side of the tank, then you blast the wall. Fractures run through the clear plastoid material. Fluid spurts. Then with a deep *crack* the whole thing gives way, spilling fluid and G'rax all over the floor.

The noise brings the guards, of course. While you help Zygash get up, you hear them running closer. You raise your blaster as they turn a corner, but you and they alike freeze at Gash's blood-curdling roar. Faster than you can believe, the G'rax's two right arms lash out to grab the lead guard's blaster rifle. The other two arms seize him and hoist him aloft like a paperweight.

The second guard fires at Zygash, but his bolt accidentally hits the first guard. As if retaliating, the first guard hits the second in return, physically, because Zygash has thrown him. Both soldiers land in a pile and lie still.

"Well, what did you need me for?" you ask Gash.

"*Hnnnrrrraaghh.*" At the warning, you turn, just in time to see the door guard enter to investigate the racket. By dropping him with one shot, you feel useful again.

Gash grabs you up in a spine-crushing grip and hugs you. "*Vnuurrgh ghuuuruugh gnaaarah!*"

Only now do you let yourself think about how much you missed him. "Same to you, buddy," you reply. "This would have been a lot lonelier galaxy without you."

With Zygash (and Wrench) by your side once more, you decide what to do with the captive Cetapod, who stares impassively from the other torture tank. Suddenly you remember the Resistance translation device.

To use the Cetapod translation device, go to 68.

19

Now that you're sure Kregg has sinister reasons for telling you his information, you actually start to relax. "So tell me more, Kregg," you say, trying to look gullible.

"Heard that G'rax left zhip, *Prozperogeneziz*, to be taken zomeplaze elze. Don't know where. But Zygash is on Pellaj, no queztion. Also have today'z Domain pazzword: 'approach vector.' Pretty nize, huh?"

"Nice, all right," you say. You make a mental note of that password, 'approach vector,' thinking that you'll probably get into deep trouble if you use it.

"What do you know about a new Domain weapon called the Subverter, Kregg?"

For a moment Kregg looks puzzled, but he quickly assumes an expression of confidence. "It'z part of big Domain zcheme on Pellaj, where Zygash iz. Go there, you find out whole workz."

"Thanks. I knew I could trust you."

You need to prevent Kregg from reporting back to—well, to whomever he reports to. Stella brings you your flask of Treesblood, and you suddenly know just how to do it. "Have a drink on me, Kregg," you say, offering the flask.

"What'z that? Treezblood? G'rax drink. No thankz."

"I insist." Before the startled alien can react, you pour the contents of the flask down his throat. He sputters, coughs—then a dreamy, contented expression slips like a curtain down over his face. He slumps on the stool. "Treesblood is a great drink," you tell the unconscious Kregg, "but if you're not used to it, you get sleepy for a while."

Time to leave. Stella tries to collect that old debt, but you couldn't afford to pay for fourteen flasks of Treesblood anyway. So you tell her that Kregg has agreed to settle your tab.

If you visit the Resistance base, go to 26.
If you want to leave the planet Silverlight, go to 45.

20

A bad, bad situation! You search desperately for repair tools, while the *Rustbucket*'s antique computer makes a damage report that goes on much too long.

Drawing on your years of piloting experience, you jury-rig repairs for the gyroscopics and the introverters. The life-support can wait; in another few moments you may not need it. But the left stabilizer is totally shot and the ship is shaking harder by the moment. How can you fix it when there's nothing on hand but wire-clippers and an obsolete lifesuit?

You try a hasty repair of the ship's stabilizer. Then a thought strikes you: the thruster! You don't need it, hurtling toward the sun as you are, but with a careful touch, you can apply enough thrust to stabilize the flight-path, like the attitude jets of ancient times. But with the gas-plumes of the primary billowing around you, do you have what it takes to do it?

At just the right moment after you zoom past the star, you hit the inertial eDrive control. Nothing happens. You age half a lifetime. Then, the familiar haziness as space gives way to eSpace—and you're on your way! The old unit just had a longer kickup than you're used to.

You use the time in eSpace to recover. Once your heartbeat goes back to normal and you get the life-support unit to give you more oxygen, you can think about the experience. It was like a trip back in time to the era when pilots flew "with nothing but sweat and star charts," as the saying goes. What heroes they were! Now that you're through the ordeal, you decide you wouldn't have missed it for the galaxy.

If you are headed for Dvaad, go to 58.
If you are headed for Pellaj, go to 10.

21

A spaceport, offices, armories, data-bank networks, mineral processing factories, navigation stations, corridors, barracks, mess-halls, and supply bureaus—Baron Jorth's stronghold, the *Ocean Lord*, is a city on the water. One of the Domain's proudest achievements, it is larger than the capital cities of many planets. In one of the Domain's infinite cruelties, this grand structure serves as an instrument of evil.

You stand in a colossal atrium, one of many on the *Ocean Lord*. Pellaj's sun shines down through banks of slanted windows, casting long bands of light across a gleaming white floor. Hundreds of inhabitants, technicians and bureaucrats and robots, walk (or wheel or float) past you. Banks of antigrav elevators line the walls.

What a slug-rat's nest, you think. Not that it's ugly, but what a labyrinth of corridors and access tunnels! Gash could be a blaster's shot away and you wouldn't know. How are you to find him in this enormous city?

A terminal nearby is labeled INFORMATION. When the Domain says INFORMATION, it means propaganda and public relations. Domain info-tapes put the best face on their abuses and conceal their atrocities. The tapes are weapons in the war for the galaxy's minds.

This one is no different. The terminal is showing a recent Domain victory as you approach. The screen shows a gigantic Cetapod being taken prisoner by a fleet of warships on the open sea. An announcer's voice: "Another leader of the so-called Resistance falls to overwhelming Domain might. Haurrassith, leader of the seagoing Cetapods race, now awaits questioning aboard the great Baron Jorth's stronghold." The announcer's ominous tone confirms the tape's implied message: *Resist the Domain, and you'll be next.*

The scene shifts to a torture tank—and you freeze. "Although some are taken by force, other fighters realize their error and make efforts to atone. Here you see a G'rax, once prominent in the Resistance, now rejoining the Domain as a loyal servant."

And there he is. Zygash stands guard over the rebel Cetapod's torture tank, with Domains beside him.

"The G'rax will help crush the Resistance by his former allies, and the Cetapod will soon provide information that will lead to the defeat of the Resistance on Pellaj. Long live the Domain!"

You almost draw your blaster and blow away the terminal. But you restrain yourself just in time. Gash was brainwashed, all right. But this only confirms your resolve to find him.

Well, this has at least given you a lead. You call up a city map on the terminal and quickly locate the general area of the detention tanks—a large red block marked CLASSIFIED. You finger your blaster.

To head for the detention tanks, go to 32.

If you wish to follow the signal from the Resistance's hand-held tracking device, go to 5.

22

Your words calm Chasma Hoyd. "They won't eat us all? Oh, you nice man, I was so worried! It's beastly that this happened. I shall write to the manager."

But her petulance gives way to fascination as you both watch the Ilirishi, who flow together and split apart in an inhuman dance. Strange features grow and vanish across each blob. "What must they look like?" says Chasma, lost in wonder.

Eventually the creatures disappear, and she appears refreshed. "I shall tell the whole committee about this adventure when I return home. And you, you handsome man, please take this as a token of my appreciation." From her gown she draws a small bulb with a few leaves around one end. "It's a seedling of the Pellajian gaspbladder plant. Its vapors are soothing," she says, "and sometimes intoxicating in concentration. Here, try it, it's delightful!" She snaps a bulb under your nose.

You sneeze violently, six times. Then your legs grow weak and you fall to your knees. "Oh, dear, oh, dear," Chasma says, flustered again. "You must be one of the rare ones who are allergic."

"Th-Thanks anyway," you choke out. You hope the Domain never learns of your new weakness. Then you retire to your cabin for a long schedule of steam inhalants, medicine, and sleep. By the time you recover, the loudspeaker announces that Pellaj lies straight ahead.

Go to 10.

23

Wrench stands in the yacht cabin, between you and Jorth. You catch the robot's eye (or photoreceptor) and gesture toward the Domain governor. You know you're in a bad spot when you have to rely on the cleverness of a robot!

Wrench waves a pincer and rolls over to Jorth.

"Excuse me, sir, shall I clean your blaster?"

"Get away!" Jorth hisses, still covering Zygash with the weapon. Wrench circles around to the far side of the cabin. "Pardon me for standing here, sir, but I'll have to be handy to clean up the blood if you slaughter Mister Zygash."

Jorth waves the blaster furiously at Wrench, and that's when you jump him. You're in a fight with Baron Jorth!

Go to 28.

24

Time is too important to waste in bantering. You grab a few folds of Kregg's stained sun-coat and pull him off his stool. "Come on, you little wart, give me the truth, or I'll space you, so help me!"

The small alien's drink goes flying and his eyes go wide. "H-Hayl—?" Then a two-clawed hand slams down on your shoulder, and you remember Stella the bartender. *"Da-snoosh, blobble Hayl!"* says the Vhurrg. But you're too angry to let Kregg go. You try throttling the little creep, find yourself being throttled, and before you know it, you're fighting the barkeep.

Stella hasn't kept this bar going so long by avoiding fights. She grabs you in both clawed hands and sends you sliding down the bar into a pile of dirty flasks.

"Na-blaggah, Hayl! Mogo dolliga blaggah, zoop!"

"All right, you don't have to get nasty," you say, rising unsteadily. You look down at the broken flasks. Stella will probably just add those to your tab. The embarrassing part is that nobody in the crowded tavern notices the fight at all. The Throbbing Throm Band hasn't even stopped playing!

This, more than anything, fills you with anger. If you're going to all this trouble for Zygash, then at least people should have the decency to notice! You grit your teeth, hitch up your leggings, and move forward.

What follows is not pretty. At least, you're fairly sure it wouldn't be pretty if you could remember it. The next time you look around, you're leaning against the bar, panting, over Stella's unconscious form. How in the Galaxy did you destroy four barstools, a row of flasks, and the keg of treesblood? Well, Stella will just add it to your tab.

Kregg is cowering behind a far table. You go over and lift him up by the nape of his sweaty sun-coat. "You've been feeding me a line, Kregg." Your look says the rest.

"Ha—Hayl, lizten. I told you truth, only the way Domain zaid to zay it. Lizten, Hayl, I make it up to you now! They wanted me to tell you pazzword: 'approach vector.' You use that pazzword, you caught. I tell you good now, okay?"

Kregg's too cowardly to bluff now. You make a mental note of that password, "approach vector," thinking it will get you in trouble if you use it.

The bad news is that the Domain knows you're here, and who knows what they're planning next? You must leave Silverlight immediately.

Go to 45.

25

Zygash is all right, but you still have to find the *Prosperogenesis*. And what was it that brainwashed Gash in the first place? The Domain has a new secret weapon called "the Subverter." The weapon can reach across interstellar distances to individual

minds, turning them into willing slaves of the
Domain. Apparently Gash was an easy target for a
trial run; maybe the Subverter finds G'rax brains
more pliable than human ones.

Zygash says the Subverter is on Dvaad, a small
asteroid mine in this system. A robot pilot took the
Genesis there, too, because the station's research labs
want to figure out how you modified your ship for
such incredibly high speeds.

Of course Gash is furious, and wants to go to
Dvaad himself to get revenge for his brainwashing.
"No, buddy," you tell him. "The Subverter knows
your mind. You can't risk going into this place. You'd
jeopardize the whole mission."

Gash is stubborn, but over your long career you've
gotten good at persuading him. He finally allows you
to go after the *Genesis* alone. Or rather, with Wrench
the maintenance bot.

First, you need a new ship. That means you need a
big favor from Tandon Rey, commander of the human
Resistance on Pellaj.

Tandon must be a great military leader to have
become commander. As he walks you along a line of
Resistance vessels, in a maintenance port beneath the
ocean surface, you decide that he sure didn't get pro-
moted because of a talent for diplomacy.

"Well, Hayl, I like you, and I'd love to give you one
of our finest ships so you can explode in style on your
suicide mission," says Tandon Rey. "But I can't sacrifice a good cruiser."

"Listen, Tandon, they told me Pellaj was a suicide
mission, too." His lack of faith—after all you've
done!—frustrates you. But as usual, the frustration
just makes you cocky. "I don't need one of your
fancy-schmancy glitzmobiles with heads-up displays
and five kinds of lifeboats! I can get to Dvaad flying
anything that holds air! You know why, Tandon?

Because I'm—"

"—just the pilot for this beauty here," he cuts in, pointing to a beat-up antique courier ship. You can't decide whether its patched belly looks sillier than its radiator fins, but they're both pretty awful. There was one of these junkheaps on Silverlight, there's one here, and there's probably one decaying in every spaceport throughout the less civilized systems. And they're all given the name *Rustbucket*.

"Happy to give you a chance to show your stuff, Hayl," says Tandon. He slaps you on the shoulder and escapes while you're still in shock. You have no choice. After some very half-hearted preparation, you climb into this deathtrap and blast off for Dvaad.

Go to 58.

26

You visit the Resistance's primary base on Silverlight, a neglected maintenance building far across the spaceport. You have some difficulty with the password robot at the entrance, and more inside with Jorah, the local Resistance commander. She's convinced that Zygash has joined the Domain, and that you're not above suspicion yourself. You tell her about Duke Carabajal's new weapon, the Subverter, and she sneers in disbelief. Then you try turning on the old Hayl charm, with the usual effect; she almost slugs you.

But you finally convince Jorah and the other rebels you're still one of them. In answer to your first question, Jorah says, "Our spy aboard the Domain's orbital station tells us that a robot pilot took the *Genesis* to an asteroid mine: Dvaad, a little Domain operation in the Dalorvan Minor system."

So you have a destination, and (after some

haggling) a ship, too: a reconditioned courier dating
from before the Circuit Wars. This relic is the only
Resistance ship that Zygash's assault didn't destroy.

Finally Jorah brings up a touchy subject. "You
know, Hayl, the Resistance needs you here. Heading
off on a rescue mission for one G'rax, even if he's
your friend—" She sees your glare and trails off.

She deserves some kind of explanation. "He's
more than my friend," you tell her. "Gash's family
raised me on their homeworld of Carelax. His elder
hearthlord adopted me as a member of their Reverence Line. That means any of them would make any
sacrifice *for* me, and they deserve the same commitment *from* me. The Resistance is important, sure,
but nothing's more important than my Reverence
Line." You look at her sheepishly, embarrassed at
your own passion. "Do you know what I'm talking
about?"

Jorah stares back. "No," she says, finally, "I don't
think I can know. But maybe I understand." She
smiles.

And then—

You hear no alarm. The sentries are as surprised as
you and Jorah. The base's reinforced door blows
inward with a colossal crash! Black smoke billows
into the room! Through the inky clouds storm
armored Imperial soldiers with full-face visors. The
leader shouts, "No prisoners!"

A dozen guerrillas fall in a shower of blaster bolts
as the soldiers storm the base. With your own weapon
in your hand before you know it, you think: *Kregg*.
The stoolie turned you in to the Domain!

Falling back behind the dismantled ships, you and
the surviving fighters fire on the invaders. The air
glows with the heat of blaster fire. Countless bolts of
red and green light scorch the walls and floor. One
strikes a handsbreadth from you, and the concrete

floor sizzles.

You drop two or three soldiers yourself, but there are too many, and no way to escape! It looks bad. . . .

You catch sight of a pile of ship weapons, stowed against the near wall while the ships are repaired and refitted. You get a crazy idea. If only those weapons haven't been powered down!

Blaster shots explode around you, rebels scream, but amid the chaos you draw a careful sight on those weapons.

The power pack of a modern weapon has a high ignition temperature. It takes concentrated blaster fire to ignite a pack. This is an important safety feature, because when a pack explodes, the blast can cover a huge area. Of course, if the pack has been powered down, it won't explode no matter how much energy you pump into it.

Your shot hits true. The bolt leaves a red glow on the pack housing, a glow that quickly fades. Nothing! Ducking another volley of blasts from the soldiers, you try again. Hit it at the same point . . . Bull's-eye! A red glow—it starts to fade—

The explosion deafens you. Shrapnel flies over your head and buries itself inches deep in a wall. Soldiers drop by the dozens, and the survivors fall back in a panic, thinking you have heavy weaponry.

"Evacuate!" Jorah shouts, and the Resistance pulls back to the rear of the building, where skimmers— sleek two-person gravity vehicles—are warmed up and ready for just such emergencies. A hatch blows open and guerrillas spread across the spaceport tarmac in all directions, evading pursuit.

"You need a ship, Hayl! Hangar bay 88!" Jorah shouts to you, moments before she zooms away. You take one of the last skimmers and whisk across the expanse toward the main hangar, seconds ahead of the soldiers. You know where to find the beat-up courier ship that the guerrillas named *Rustbucket*. It isn't the ship you'd prefer, but the time for choices has passed.

Zigzagging to dodge enemy bolts, you leave a sinuous cloud of dust in your wake. You jump the skimmer over the entrance guardrails and *into* the spaceport hangar, then sound the horn to warn crewmen and repair robots out of your path. You pull up by hangar bay 88 just as the Domain troops hit the entrance behind you.

Stealing a look at the ship before you leap up the open gangway, you think, *I'll never get this clunker off the ground!* It's a dirty, dented, decrepit tin can with belly patches and radiator fins. But you jump into the cockpit anyway.

There's a maintenance robot in the hold, a standard MRP model. Wait, you know this bot—it's Wrench!

"Hello, Captain Hayl. You appear to be in mortal danger again."

"Wrench, how did you get here? Never mind, I'm in a hurry!" Going through the endless warmup sequence, you wonder what's holding up the pursuers. Then you see. Looks like the crewmen in the hangar don't like the Domain any more than you do, because they're "directing" the troopers down blind alleys and after ghostly quarries. By the time the soldiers find your skimmer, you're ready to zoom, and air clearance be hanged!

The launch is deafening. The gravity wavers sickeningly. You wish you'd had a chance to haul a better maintenance robot along in this contraption, but it's too late now. You blast away, leaving Silverlight a slim, silvery crescent behind you.

After a few minutes you catch your breath. You turn to Wrench. "Talk."

"I knew you wanted to clear Master Zygash's name, Captain Hayl. I assumed you would eventu-

ally come to the Resistance base for clues, and I was right."

"But why did you come after me?"

"You own me now, sir."

"Me?"

"When the G'rax pilot blasted off without warning, your ship did great damage to the equipment around it. The spaceport has collected the insurance bond you posted and written off the equipment, including me."

"Well, such a deal," you say bitterly. The bond could have bought a dozen MRP units. Still, in the years since you joined the Resistance, money has become less important to you. Slightly.

"Are you up for a dangerous trip, Wrench?"

"Indeed I am, sir. You left me at the *Prosperogenesis* hangar bay before I could volunteer to help you. I have served you and Master Zygash for only a short time, but you are better masters than most. I would feel honored to help you in your cause. Or, if you fail, it will be an honor to clean your blood from wherever it spills."

You swallow. "That's a touching sentiment, Wrench. You do have a way with words. Well, see if you can keep this junkheap together long enough to find Gash." You turn to the job of plotting a course.

Go to 2.

27

"Hey, keep your armor on, okay?" you tell the sentry, waving your hand soothingly. "I don't want in, I'm just passing by." You and Wrench stroll past him down the sunlit corridor.

You find no other entrance, but you notice one small ventilation hatch high up on a wall.

"Wait here, Wrench," you tell the robot.

"Yes, sir. If you happen to die in there, let me put your mind at ease: I can easily take up duties here after you're gone."

"Thanks so much for calming me on that point." Leaving Wrench below, you float upward with no more than a slight whine from the antigrav belt. You pry away a vent grate and enter.

You're in a webwork of catwalks and gantryways near the ceiling of an enormous room. From this catwalk you can make out sounds of conversation—and sounds of pain. But it's impossible to get a decent view. You float silently down and land gently behind a bank of machinery.

Go to 18.

28

You struggle with Jorth on the deck of the yacht. A little wretch like this guy should drop with one punch, you think, and draw back your fist. You strike—

—Jorth rolls out of the way, faster than you can see. His right cross takes you in the jaw, and it feels like the whole ship fell on you. Jorth leaps to his feet and laughs. "You are not quite ready for a worthy opponent, Hayl, yes?"

You shake your head back and forth, thinking, How did this fat slug-rat get so strong? Must have been a lucky punch. You stagger toward him, ready for anything—

When he throws you against a bulkhead, you take part of his sleeve with you. On Jorth's exposed arm you see the skeletal braces, the network of vanadium wires, and the servomotors bulging at the elbow and shoulder.

"Powersheath!" you shout to Gash.

Jorth is rich indeed, to afford the motorized exoskeleton that must have cost nearly as much as this space-yacht. At the sight of the deadly power-sheath, Zygash leaps at Jorth. But with a sideswipe of his powered arm, the governor strikes at the G'rax's throat. Gash falls to the deck and does not move.

You're alone against a vastly more powerful foe. You don't dare engage him directly. Backing up as he walks slowly toward you, you look for something to throw at him. But a spacecraft, even a luxury space-craft, doesn't have loose furniture.

"You are trapped, Hayl. You have no means of escape. There is nowhere to run."

"You sure are repetitive, Jorth," you say absently, looking around. "You say the same thing over and over. You keep restating the same idea. You are a repetitive person." There! You see a glimmer of hope, but taking advantage of it will require perfect timing.

"Backing up against a wall, Hayl? I am surprised," says Jorth, looking like a Carelaxian mantis-cat toying with a bug. "You should have kept to the open area, where you could have run a bit longer before I dismembered you."

" 'Dismembered,' that's good, Jorth. It has three whole syllables. Want to try for four?" You position yourself by an inconspicuous wall panel. Behind the panel you hear the gurgle of fluids.

Jorth does not try for four syllables. Instead, your taunts have the effect you wanted, and with a wordless cry of anger he draws back and punches at you. Move—he's too fast! His fist slams into your shoulder. Despite yourself, you cry out in pain.

"Hahhh! Where is the Hayl wit now?" Jorth draws back for another punch. This is it, now or never! With speed born of fear, you twist aside just as the punch lands. It would have hit your throat; instead—

Jorth's hand, gloved in metal harder than a ship's hull, punches straight through the thin wall panel. Tubes snap, and from the hole squirt streams of boiling water and Kr'ilysian singflower tea. The hot liquids hit Jorth right in his unprotected face. He screams!

His powered arms whip up to cover his face. Dazed by the pain, Baron Jorth forgets his own strength. His hands strike like mallets, snapping his head back with force stronger than your best punch. He falls to the deck, stunned.

You waste no time deactivating the suit and peeling away the power packs. "Just want you to know, Jorth," you tell the still form, "that's the first time today I've beat someone using a beverage dispenser."

You, Gash, and Wrench take the unconscious Baron Jorth back to the Resistance fighters on Pellaj, for ransom or other disposition as they see fit. Then you're ready to leave the planet.

If you have already been to the Dvaad asteroid mine in this adventure, go to 93.
If you have not yet gone to Dvaad, go to 38.

29

The Hotjets bar has gone downhill since you last got thrown out. But you know this grubby dome is still the hangout for the little alien stoolie Kregg. Inside, through the smoky air, you can see Stella the Vhurrg bartender, still blue and scaly but now with one less eye than last time. Bartending must be a tough life.

"Stella!" you cry, over the raucous music of a thrommer band. "Seen Kregg anywhere around?"

"*Ho glabbor na yoggit hoggoosh smooze.*"

"Oh, no! How long ago?"

"*Ihh . . . snorble. Ogo snorble.*"

Blast! If Kregg has gone to the flesh pits, you know you won't see him today (at least!). And you can't think of another reliable stoolie around the spaceport area. Waiting here would take too long. Besides, it looks as if Stella has recognized you, and is mentioning a big drinks-and-damage tab you ran up on your last visit.

As you edge out the door, smiling at Stella all the while, you bump into a tall, dapper human with piercing eyes. He politely sidesteps you and saunters into the bar. Out of Stella's sight, you listen at the door as the man makes an announcement: "Attention, potential travelers! I, a humble space miner, seek companionship for a journey to Dvaad, the asteroid mine in the Dalorvan Minor system. Those interested in applying for passage aboard my vessel, passage which, I stress, is free of cost, should report to hangar bay 45 before the day is out. Thank you. You may resume your drunken revelry."

This must be—what was that name you saw at the registry? Jaspon Dentoze?

If you inquire about passage with Jaspon Dentoze, go to 37.

If you want to leave Silverlight, go to 45.

30

You check the *Rustbucket*'s faded computer screen. Like any Resistance ship, it has a whole library of fake names and clearance codes. Scrolling through them, you can't tell which ones have been compromised and which are still safe—but they all look old, and the coding equipment is none too modern, either. Getting clearance to land is too dangerous. You'll just have to go in the hard way.

You know from experience that asteroid security monitors have to correct their orbits constantly. There's no stable orbit around an irregular chunk of rock the size of a city. From a safe distance, you scout the monitor orbits, waiting for a minor security gap to appear as they drift out of place.

You try not to remember the only reason anyone tolerates such minor holes: No sane pilot would possibly try to fly a ship through them. And here you are trying to do it in the *Rustbucket*!

You spot a characteristic drift in one probe's orbit. It won't be long before the attitude jets correct it, so you have to dive in fast.

Two probes fade over Dvaad's horizon; it's wide open. You move in fast; maybe they'll mistake you for a meteor. The asteroid grows from a ball to a landscape, and then a new probe appears on the horizon. If it detects you, you're cooked. You have to get out of sight!

With a twist of the throttle, you send the *Rustbucket* screaming toward a high, rocky ridge. A sheer stone wall rises before you, and you slam the controls. The ship rocks in protest, and the console lights up red. No time to check the malfunctions because the ground is coming up fast.

You barely manage to bottom out—no you don't, because a rocky outcropping sticks out from the ridge right in your path. It would have no business being there on a higher-gravity world. Here it sweeps away your top maneuvering jets, and you slam into the ground.

When you wake up, the pressure alarms are ringing. Hull leak! But outside it's dark—where are you? Switching on the landing lights, you find you've crashed through Dvaad's crust into a deserted mining tunnel. Your console shows there's a thin atmosphere out there. With its left wingfoil shot and the landing gear simply gone, the *Rustbucket* isn't leaving Dvaad ever again. But you're unhurt, and you weren't planning to leave without the *Genesis* anyway.

The pressure in the tunnel is low but adequate, just like the air in most asteroids. You venture down the dark, echoing tunnel.

Tendrils of mist curl around your feet. Echoes of machinery reach you. From what you know of asteroid acoustics, the echoes could be coming from down this tunnel, or from the far side of this world. With your own breathing loud in your ears, you feel very much alone in a faraway place.

Out of the mist a little alien creature races toward you. It's a knee-high insectile thing with a ridged white shell and many legs. It's making sounds like *chik, chuk*. You pull your blaster and leap out of its way—and it scuttles past, ignoring you. "Well, glad to meet you too, I guess," you mutter. You keep walking.

After a short time you come to a branch in the tunnel,

with dim light at the end of each branch. From the left path come sounds of machinery—and human voices! From the right, you hear strange noises like the insect-thing made: *chi-chaukkachuk, kutchakutcha, chikitch*.

If you go left, go to 17.
If you go right, go to 84.

31

Better get this rattling courier down on solid ground as soon as possible. Surveying the atoll from overhead, you note its low profile approvingly. It's hardly more than a sandbar on the surface, though the reef beneath must be gargantuan. Given its rough surface, the walking will be risky. Good thing your boots are genuine Carelaxian grufflump leather.

You see no sign of danger from horizon to horizon as you bring the *Rustbucket* in for a remarkably smooth landing. You look out the viewport at some puzzling smooth patches on the atoll. Suddenly you think, This is no atoll!

Vrroomph! At that same instant, the entire ship tilts to one side, throwing you against a bulkhead. The atoll moves beneath you. You've landed the *Rustbucket* on the back of a Cetapod! The ship splashes into the ocean and sinks like a rock. Instantly you hear a warning trickle of water from a leaky bulkhead—maybe several bulkheads.

Whew! You hadn't realized just how *big* these creatures are. The titanic creature fills your whole viewport. It's a floating black wall, and then a bulging cylinder, and finally a gaping mouth lined with teeth.

Does the thing even know you're here? If it had wanted to hurt you, it would have attacked already. It might still accidentally destroy the *Rustbucket* with a casual swipe of its tail. You have to alert this thing that you exist.

You search the unfamiliar console for a loud-speaker switch—nothing! If this contraption even has a public-address speaker, you can't find it.

The *Rustbucket*'s laser is a moldy old model that went out with the Circuit Wars. It wouldn't do more than scratch this Cetapod's barnacled black hide. A warning shot, then.

You fire a garnet-red beam wide of the creature's head. The beam sets the water boiling with its heat, and the bubbles seem to startle the Cetapod. It swims away with amazing speed. You realize it must have hit you by accident.

The creature's powerful tail strokes buffet your ship, even from far away. The *Rustbucket* springs a few more leaks. You have to do something soon.

While you debate your choices, the Cetapod stops in the distance. You see its silhouette, with the bulging midsection and the clusters of tentacles on the head. Then you see human swimmers! The Cetapod is chasing them—no, they're streaming from the creature's mouth!

Jetting toward you and flashing Resistance arm-signals, the frogmen call you over the commlink. "Step outside, Hayl, the water's fine!"

Sounds like a good idea. The *Rustbucket* has an emergency breather mask in its bailout box. The bailout box is about all that still works on the founder-ing ship.

"Are you waterproof, Wrench?" you ask the robot.

A billowing sheet of plastic erupts from Wrench's boxy waist. It expands into a bubble and seals itself around the bot. "I am now, sir."

You and Wrench emerge from the main airlock into the warm water. Hanging there weightless, with green water above and the black depths beneath, you feel like you're hanging in space. Your ship sinks toward the bottom, kilometers below, growing smaller and smaller. At least you won't have to fly that heap again.

Then you wonder whether you should have gone down with your ship, because the Resistance swimmers want you to follow them into the Cetapod's gaping mouth! If that doesn't test your commitment to the cause, nothing will.

Not believing them at first, you watch as the swimmers pass ahead of you. With a few strokes of their foot fins, they propel themselves toward the long curving line of the creature's jaw. Hesitantly you follow, dragging Wrench in his inflated bubble. Any moment now they'll stop and say it was just a test. Any moment. Any—

The gigantic mouth opens and water rushes in, carrying you along. Pulled toward the waiting blackness, you feel you're falling, falling into empty space, faster and faster . . . In your breather mask you begin to scream.

You're swallowed like a tidbit, get squeezed through the Cetapod's throat along with a torrent of water, and wash into a foul-smelling stomach. Gasping, you look around. Where's that light coming from? Whose hand is that stretching toward you? *What's going on?*

Go to 6.

32

You walk along these corridors as though you know where you are going, hoping the guards watching the surveillance monitors think the same. Well, at least the security here is less than that on some other

Domain bases you've seen. These are open corridors, with entrances guarded by individual soldiers. Maybe Baron Jorth didn't rate major Domain funding.

Or maybe the Domain thinks no one could possibly be crazy enough to march into a prison, unarmored, with nothing but a blaster, to break out a friend. Yeah, that must be it. You've seen more than your share of Domain detention areas, and not a single one ever made casual visitors feel welcome.

Your feet are getting sore. How far have you walked? Suddenly you stop, aching feet forgotten, as you hear a G'rax roar in the distance.

You walk on, fighting not to break into a run. After a couple of turns you come to a sunlit corridor with a high ceiling. One Domain guard stands sentry at the single door in the hall; his dark body armor absorbs the sunlight. Vents of some kind line the high wall to your left. In the long right window another part of the *Ocean Lord* stretches away like a monstrous tentacle.

There it is again. The distinctive harmonic roar of a G'rax—Zygash! The roar comes from this room, along with a lot of strange sounds like blaster shots and bubbling. As you keep walking toward the door, the sentry's grip tightens on his deadly Kelimar V blaster rifle. With his armor and blastproof full-face visor, he looks genuinely tough, and you know he'll want a password. What's worse, a surveillance camera high on the opposite wall monitors him.

If you have already been to the Dvaad asteroid mine in this adventure, go to 39. If you have not gone to Dvaad yet, choose one of these:

To try tricking the guard, go to 44.
To use your antigrav harness, go to 47.
If you want to give a password, go to 92.

33

"Uh, this is the *Small Waist*," you say over the radio to the control tower. "Here to pick up a load of—uh—cargo. Request landing clearance." You activate the ship's security code transmitter.

"ID confirmed, *Small Waist*," says the controller. "Prepare to land on following approach vector."

Another voice breaks in. "Say, Dentoze, got any shirts for us?" You can hear the laughter in the background. No wonder the miner went crazy.

You get immediate clearance to touch down at what passes for the spaceport. From above it's nothing but a flattened patch of bare rock, blackened with the scorch marks of a thousand launches. Then a lighted docking port opens in the ground, and you descend neatly into the underground mining colony.

As the bay doors close over your ship and air floods the bay, you see a long line of soldiers passing in formation before an observation window. Not just any soldiers, either—it looks like about a battalion of Elite Imperial Soldiers, all armed to the face-visors. Soldiers, on a mining colony! Something deeply strange is happening here on Dvaad.

Go to 84.

34

You leap for a standing rack of tubes, vials, and tanks. Bending low and holding your breath, as you have many times in your checkered career, you hide behind the rack—just as three technicians enter the lab.

"Hnnnhh," groans one. "Back to this hyper unit. What a mess! Did you see this one, Borlis? It's from that Marauder clunker in the hangar down the hall."

"Yeah," another replies. "Looks like it was hand tooled with parts from twenty different models." (Only eleven, you think.) "You gurks figured out what makes it go yet?"

"We're just about to start the teardown," says the third. "Give us time!"

The techs are heading for your eDrive unit with wrenches and pry bars. For a moment you're afraid you'll have to jump them, but a signal from outside distracts them. "Dinner break!" says one eagerly. They all rush out. As you emerge from hiding, you wonder how the Domain manages to stay around when its servants keep taking breaks.

You retrieve your eDrive system and take it back to the *Genesis*, waiting in its hangar nearby.

Go to 73.

35

While the other Worldways passengers line up at the customs gate, you slip down a gangway and through the galley to the supply loading ports. Good—the whole crew is busy, and you easily disarm their kid-stuff alarms.

"How much farther, Captain Hayl?" says Wrench.

"Shhh!"

"Oh," it says quietly. "This is some illicit activity, I take it. You may count on my full cooperation."

"Shut up, Wrench." You both sneak out onto a concrete canopy, past a detail of loadbots.

"Halt!" comes a mechanical voice. You turn to see a tall, shiny cylinder, mounted on speed-treads and bristling with weapons and surveillance devices: a security robot. It's spotted you.

" 'Scuse me," you tell the security robot, "I gotta

get the Area Foreman. Foodmaker blowup in the galley, we got lotsa spoiled food in that place, wheeew! You smell it?"

"I do not have olfactory sensors. Stand still while I radio for an escort squad."

Blast! You don't want to tangle with a Domain security robot in the best of circumstances, but on this open canopy, with no cover, you almost decide to give up. Then Wrench says, "Say, you've got a nice polish. I've tried and tried to get my zirconium to shine like that."

"You like it?" preens the security robot. "The Merpie unit over there did this for me. Do you know him?"

"No, but we all strive to clean the best we can. That's our job."

After a few moments of pleasant robot talk, you break in to mention that you'd like to take "your little metal buddy" into the stronghold for repair. The security robot quickly escorts you to—sigh!—the customs area you wanted to dodge.

"Can't leave my post," the bot tells you, "but take your friend to the repair bay on Blue Deck. Tell them Slaughterman Number 443-F sent you."

"Thanks," you say, not even trying to sound sincere.

Go to 82.

36

The Subverter speaks in your mind. *Come here, humanbeing, that we may merge.* Before you realize it, you're walking with jerky steps toward the hive-mind. The voice says, *Open its mouth,* and you open your mouth. A dozen Kakklakks climb your body, spray hot goo in your face, and one sticks its filament-thin legs up your nostrils and down your throat. In an instant the powerful alien mind is raiding your memories.

This is a primitive intellect, it thinks. *The device is not complex*. The insects fall away, leaving you gasping. While you wipe away the slime, Kakklakks pick up parts of the *Genesis*. They carry the pieces, one at a time, out the hangar exit.

"Whah—where are they going?"

"I have no idea, sir," says Wrench.

Hundreds of Kakklakks remain in the hive-mind, directing the others. The Subverter speaks. *Ship must be taken to surface. We put it together again there.*

Speechless, you watch the hordes. You see more all the time, including new types you haven't seen before—big, lumbering brutes with tufts of hair growing between their shell ridges.

Harvester caste, the Subverter explains. *We reap the growths deep within the world that feed the cattle. These can carry ship's larger pieces.*

"Well," you say, bemused, "I give you credit for enthusiasm. But not even a regiment of those harvesters can carry the *Genesis* hull."

Incorrect. Now you notice many bugs crawling slowly across the hull. They drip lines of yellow fluid from their abdomens. Behind them, the trails of fluid smoke and sizzle.

"Acid—hey! They're cutting apart my ship! You've got to stop them, now!"

But the Subverter says nothing. The carving continues. Pieces of your ship fall with a crash, often crushing Kakklakks in the fall. You groan in pain, but the hive-mind ignores you. Harvesters hoist the chunks of metal onto their broad backs and trudge out the exit.

After an eternity of suffering, you gaze on an empty hangar. You remark inanely, "You've carried away my ship."

Correct. Proceed to the surface of the world. Humanbeing requires lifesuit, found elsewhere in this area. Controlled by the Subverter almost as an afterthought, you go to the hangar's supply cabinet and don a lifesuit, then follow the creatures up a slanting tunnel. Wrench wheels along behind you. After a long walk through misty passages, you and Wrench emerge in bright starlight on the surface of Dvaad.

The asteroid looks bleak, brown, rocky, irregular, and covered with parts of the *Prosperogenesis*. Kakklakks wander among them, unaffected by the rigors of space. The hive-mind has reformed here, and you hear its thoughts in your mind.

We have gathered the principles of ship from humanbeing's limited understanding. We now commence reassembly. Certain elements of the design are inefficient. Does it wish us to redesign ship?

You cannot speak aloud up here on the surface, but you think, *No! Make it just like it was!* You feel like you're arguing with yourself.

It is irrelevant to our needs that the humanbeing desires inefficiency. We will comply.

They do. The harvesters lift the hull pieces into place, while other workers exude a fluid of lighter yellow. It fuses the metal pieces together with hardly a seam. Guided in mysterious ways by the hive-mind, hundreds of Kakklakks carry the parts aboard. You can tell from experience that they bring the parts in proper order, with uncanny speed and precision. All of them serve one intellect, just as your own hands and feet serve yours.

Before long you stare openmouthed at the reassembled *Prosperogenesis*. The Subverter has done the work of a dozen robots, over maybe ten shifts, in the time you took to use one tank of air from the emergency lifesuit!

The gangway lowers, and you and Wrench enter the ship. Scads of natives swarm around your feet. The *Genesis* cabin is lighted, her circuits all in place. Looking around, you can't tell that anything untoward ever happened to her. *Thanks*, you think.

Then it says, *We are on ship, as many as will fit. The humanbeing will take us to another Kakklakk colony now.* You look at the piles of natives, pulsing and writhing, filling every available space in the cabin. Yet there are still dozens or hundreds crawling around outside.

You close the gangway, pressurize the cabin, and go forward to the cockpit. "What about the rest of you guys?" you ask the Subverter.

We who remain behind will not live in the Dukebeing's control. Humanbeing will ignite its thrusters now.

A little dazed, you run through the familiar launch sequence. When you warm up the thrusters, you look out a viewport. The Kakklakks that remained outside are marching single file into the ship's exhaust, where they silently burn to crisps. *It is the way and the rhythm of ten million orbits*, says the voice in your mind. Actually, the loss of those individual members of the hive-mind must mean no more than the loss of a fingernail or drop of blood means to you. Still, you shiver.

Blasting into space, you wonder how to get by the orbital defenses you encountered on the way in. In fact, an automatic probe spots you and lets loose with blaster fire—fire that falls on your ship and bounces away!

The Subverter must be protecting you, but how? Then you remember its mastery of the Music of the Spheres. The Music can protect as well as destroy.

The voice in your mind says, *The Music sounds everywhere louder than the humanbeings' weapons. We will not be bothered again.*

You fly into the asteroid belt. Piloting around the onrushing rocks is tight work, but you feel your

reflexes operating at inhumanly high levels. The Subverter seems to follow a particular course, and soon you arrive at a large asteroid that looks, outwardly, like the one you left, or any other. *Here we reach our destiny*, comes the thought. You land smoothly.

The hive-mind speaks from its many mouths as it departs. *Here is another colony. We enter, to merge and die. The young will know the Domain, the Dukebeing, and the humanbeing's Resistance. But they will not permit any further contact. They will live undetected on their worlds, and drift until they find new colonies. It is—*

"Yeah, the way and rhythm of ten million orbits, I know. What about me? What about my friend Gash?"

The humanbeing cannot track the world's orbit after the merging. The world will explode, carrying our many young on new orbits. Therefore, we allow the humanbeing to leave alive.

"Gee, thanks."

*The Subverter, as the Dukebeing knew it, is no more.
The otherbeing Zygash is free of influence. A fascinating
mind, less primitive than the humanbeing's.* You're glad
Gash isn't around to hear that; you'd never live it
down.

You evacuate the cabin, the natives file out the
gangway, and they enter a nearby tunnel leading
deep into the asteroid. You blast off once more,
quickly leave the hazards of the asteroid belt behind,
and gaze back at the little tumbling world. After you
watch for a while, the asteroid blows up with a bright
flash, carrying its little colonies on new paths
throughout the system. Ah, romance, you think.

If you have already visited Pellaj, go to 93.
If you have not yet gone to Pellaj, go to 67.

37

At hangar bay 45 you find a tall, slender man
dressed stylishly in a tan slacksuit with black piping.
A cream-colored ascot adorns his throat, and an aris-
tocratic expression marks his features. "Ah, hello.
Were you one of those in that beastly bar earlier—?"
he asks, then goes on without pause. "Well, it hardly
matters. Jaspon Dentoze is my name. I am a miner by
trade." He offers his hand regally.

"Most of the miners I know are grizzled old geezers
who never take off their pressure suits," you say,
smiling.

"And seldom bathe. You have my sympathy. Nev-
ertheless, I am as I say. I launch shortly for the Dvaad
asteroid mine in Dalorvan Minor. I take it you are
interested in coming along?"

"Maybe. If you want someone to talk to, I'm a good
listener. If you want to listen, I've got stories enough

to last to the other end of the Galaxy."

"And you're reasonably clean, too. That puts you far ahead of the rabble who have applied thus far. Very well, I shall accept you as passenger. I can also use a maintenance robot, should you have one."

"Why, I do," you say, thinking of Wrench the MRP unit from the *Prosperogenesis* hangar bay. As you recall the bot, you notice how Jaspon moves in Wrench's rigid, robotic way. Whenever Jaspon looks at something, he stares fixedly. He looks spacesick.

You've met lots of eccentrics in your travels, but this Jaspon is creepy. Riding with him wouldn't necessarily be dangerous . . . but you expect to keep your blaster handy.

If you go with Jaspon Dentoze to Dvaad (bringing Wrench the robot), go to 77.

If you politely refuse and look for another way to leave Silverlight, go to 45.

38

Your launch from Pellaj goes smoothly. Baron Jorth's space-yacht has such fancy navigational equipment that it's a snap to lay in a course. Your destination: Dvaad, a small asteroid mine in the Dalorvan Minor system.

If only Zygash were with you. You had to leave him behind with the Pellaj Resistance. After he recovered from his brainwashing, he was furious, and set on revenge against the Domain. While in the Domain's service, he learned about its new secret weapon, "the Subverter." The weapon can reach across interstellar distances to individual minds, turning them into willing slaves of the Domain. Apparently Gash was an easy target for a trial run;

maybe the Subverter finds G'rax brains more pliable than human ones.

Zygash says the Subverter is located on Dvaad. The *Genesis* is there, too, because the station's research labs want to figure out how you modified your ship for such high speeds. So when you set out to retrieve your ship, you asked Gash to stay behind. "You can't risk going into this place. The Subverter knows you already. Your presence could jeopardize the whole mission."

The persuasion took a lot of talking, but Gash finally allowed you to go after the *Genesis* alone. Or rather, with Wrench, the maintenance bot.

You speed toward the mine in Jorth's luxury star-cruiser. It's not quite as fast as the *Genesis*, of course, but what a classy ride! To pass the time, you ask Wrench, "Any experience with Dvaad?"

"Not personally, sir. A maintenance robot on Silverlight had served with me in the hangar briefly. It said the mining operation was an ordinary small outfit."

As though a robot would notice anything unusual, you think.

But when you bring up Dvaad's records from the ship's database, it does indeed look typical. A holo-gram shows rounded refinery towers, waste sluices open to the vacuum of space, and the usual railgun ramp that accelerates buckets of metal to orbital fac-tories. Dirty gray domes, houses for mine personnel, cluster beneath one tower. The whole mine looks so grimy it might have grown whole from the living rock of the asteroid.

Nothing unusual. But the Domain runs Dvaad, and that makes it unusual. Ordinarily the Domain would never bother with a little operation like this.

Such equipment on this starcruiser! The mine is still just a speck of light when your high-power transmitter submits clearance codes. Of course, Baron Jorth's personal ship gets instant clearance. Blast doors slide back from a docking port, revealing a well-equipped bay.

You land as lightly as a feather. The doors close and atmosphere floods into the port. You lean back in the upholstered pilot's seat, happy things are going smoothly for a change.

Then the radio announces, "Please stand by for the welcoming party, Governor."

From every airlock in the port area, soldier honor guards march toward your ship. Martial music sounds over the PA system. An official greeting party comes out, wearing full dress regalia. They wait solemnly before the gangway entrance.

"Blowout!" you curse. What to do? You grab the mike for the ship's own PA loudhailer. "Uh, hi, everybody," you stammer. "I'm real pleased to be here. I, um, I can't come to the door right now—sick, I'm sick!"

There is commotion among the greeting party. The yacht's external mikes pick up their words. "We'll send in a medical robot at once, Governor!"

"No! Uh, no, really, no trouble, just go on with your work, and I'll be out when I feel a little better." But it's hopeless. Your refusal arouses their suspicion; they make voiceprint checks; they override your security and break in with a phalanx of soldiers. And you were doing so well, too!

On the march to the Supervisor's office, the soldiers take you and Wrench through the heart of the Dvaad mining operation. You walk through gaping tunnels, some natural, others drilled. Like many asteroids, Dvaad has a thin, breathable internal atmosphere.

You can't look around much, with your hands on your head. But you do see the usual mining-colony features: drill robots, smelters, airtight hatches, now and then a cart filled with explosives. High overhead on the tunnel ceiling, gravsleds on rails carry ore to dispatch stations or disposal chutes, unimpeded by traffic below. This is all routine.

What's unexpected are the white insectlike creatures that crawl everywhere in the tunnels. Though no higher than your knee, they move quickly on many slender legs, seemingly heading nowhere in particular. They must be natives of the asteroid.

"Who are your houseguests?" you ask a guard.

"Shut up and keep walking."

After many turns you come to a huge cavern, the administration center of the mining operation. Shabby permex-and-lockslab barracks tower overhead, and prefabricated office domes sprawl around them. One such office, less grimy than the rest, houses Supervisor Tasko.

Tasko looks like his office: small, clean, colorless. But the room, even with its security cameras and heavy, barrierlike furniture, can't capture Tasko's air of nervousness. The wiry supervisor looks haunted—not at all like your typical Domain goon. Sitting behind a shielded desk, he pets the ridged shell of a native. The creature ignores him and gnaws at a desk leg.

Tasko dismisses the guards, and you think about jumping him. But you're unarmed, the guards are outside, there are cameras—maybe later. "You were expected, of course," says Tasko. "You are here to investigate our new Subverter weapon."

"I'm here to get my ship. Give it to me, and I'll go."

"Oh, Hayl. I hardly know what to think of you. You've come to the Domain's most secret research base. Here we have developed a weapon that can turn even the most fanatical Resistance traitor into our willing slave—as happened to your friend, the G'rax. From here, we will turn your Resistance to our side, one leader at a time. And you expect me to believe you're here just to retrieve your ship?"

Tasko doesn't smile, but scratches the insectlike

native behind its faceted eyes. "Either you assume me to be, or you yourself are, no more intelligent than—well, than this single Kakklakk."

"Yeah. What is that thing?"

He shoots you a glance, then returns to scratching the chitinous shell. "The Kakklakks are natives of this asteroid. They are harmless, I assure you."

"If they're getting in your way, why don't you just exterminate them? Isn't that the way the Domain works?"

"The Domain has made many enemies that way," Tasko replies unexpectedly. "I see no point in making more. The Domain's adversaries are more numerous than it seems." He falls silent and looks at you.

You can't figure his meaning, but you hear a guilty conscience in Tasko's words. Your reply plays on his uncertainty. "And growing all the time. Join us."

Tasko stares at you for a moment, then looks nervously at the monitor camera in a corner of the ceiling. He stabs at a button on his desktop, and a red light on the camera winks out.

"Be prepared to leave suddenly tonight," he says quickly. Then he indicates silence and pushes the button again, relighting the camera before you can ask anything. "Just testing," he says to the camera.

A squad of soldiers escorts you to a cell. There you sit until lights dim in the detention block, signalling the onset of night-cycle in this part of the complex.

The door slides back, and Tasko stands there with Wrench at his side. Small, nervous, the supervisor still seems more decisive than he did before.

He calls you out and hands you a blaster. "I've sent the guards away. There's a fast courier ship warmed up in docking bay 33, with automatic launch clearance. Warn the Resistance about the Subverter. Go rescue your G'rax friend—he's in Baron Jorth's stronghold on Pellaj, in this system."

"Come with me. Duke Carabajal will want your hide for this."

"He'll get it. I can't go." For a moment his decisive manner gives way to the old, furtive look. "I'm no guerrilla. I'm not brave like you. I just want to do what I can to stop the Domain." He motions for you and Wrench to leave the detention block.

You look back once when you head into the darkened tunnels. Tasko stands small but proud in the shadows, waving you on. You don't know how he's going to explain this, or what the Domain will do to him. But the Resistance couldn't survive without such small acts of heroism.

As you near the docking bay, your mind races. You could get away—but without the *Genesis*, and without trying to stop this Subverter weapon. No, you can't let Tasko's help go for nothing. You dodge down a side-tunnel and head into the mining complex, resolved to find your ship—or the weapon—or both.

Eventually you come to a branching of tunnels. Down the left tunnel you hear the sounds of machinery. The right carries alien clicking sounds.

If you go left, go to 17.
If you go right, go to 84.

39

The sentry is waiting for a password. You feel sure you heard Zygash's roar from the room beyond. With the Subverter out of the way, Gash might still be pretending loyalty to the Domain, to protect himself. But that isn't your friend's way, which means that if he's still alive, he's in deep trouble.

You must get into that room.

To use the antigrav belt, go to 27.

If you give the password "Approach vector," go to 90.

If you give the password "Fusion furnace," go to 79.

If you try a fast-talking con job, go to 52.

40

You turn a corner to enter hangar bay 88, glance up, see the Resistance ship *Rustbucket*, and almost turn the corner in reverse. This used courier ship must date back to the Circuit Wars. Walking up its skewed gangplank, you gape at the fluidic control system, the unshielded gun pod, the inertial—*inertial!*—eDrive unit. The bulkheads have been patched so many times there's not much left but patches.

This clunker belongs in a museum, not in space. But you may not have a better choice. If you decide to take the *Rustbucket*, it's an excellent idea to bring a maintenance robot along. You'll take Wrench, the MRP bot from the *Prosperogenesis* hangar bay.

If you leave the planet Silverlight in this ship, go to 2.

If you want to leave some other way, go to 45.

41

You present Wrench to the customs inspector as "your personal valet-bot."

"Pretty clunky-looking for a valet," the inspector notes.

Yes (you start to say), if you'd known what would arrive, you never would have placed the order with that used-bot dealer. But Wrench thinks the comment is directed at him. "Oh," says the well-meaning mechanical, "really I'm good at cleaning, because that's my job. I got the *Prosperogenesis* as clean as clean before Zygash stole it. Tell him, Captain Hayl."

You're surrounded by guards before you can even think of drawing your blaster, then marched off to Baron Jorth. "You're the most heavily mixed blessing I've ever seen," you mutter to Wrench.

"Why, thank you, Captain Hayl."

"No talking!"

With soldiers behind and ahead, you walk along sunlit glass hallways, with the infinite ocean of Pellaj stretching away beyond them. Then the hallway gives way to an open landing deck, where wharves lined with seacraft thrust into the water.

The soldiers look like bored spear-carriers. This could be your chance to escape. Are you willing to dodge a few blaster shots as you run for a sea-skimmer? Of course; you're Rogan Hayl!

"Owww," you moan, starting to limp. "That old war wound, acting up." The soldiers hesitate, and your time-tested trick works again. The split-second pause lets you push through their ranks and dash for the seaside landing. A heartbeat later, blaster bolts shoot past you.

"Come on, Wrench, the ship is leaving!"

The boxy maintenance bot wheels speedily along. "This is likely to result in an awful death, Captain Hayl," it says calmly.

Dodging the weapon fire, you leap off the canopy onto a sea-skimmer, pull down the bubble hood, rev the jets, and zoom away across the ocean. Wrench grabs the rear fender with one pincer as you go, then pulls itself aboard behind you. Alarms sound, warning of the six Elite Imperial Soldiers that soon chase you.

A cloudless blue sky, a peaceful sea on a warm day—what a beautiful setting for a high-speed chase where one slip of a skimmer-foil means instant, bloody death. You skip across the waves, your jets leaving a high, foaming wake. The six Domain guards, close behind now, skip and splash across that wake in zigzag pursuit patterns.

Clutching the handlebars of the sea-skimmer, you straddle the seat and check its skimpy instrument panel. The depth indicator shows a large reef just under the surface, off to your left. Other than that, it's just you and the Domains and the wide open sea.

Already they're closer. If you keep heading straight, they'll catch you.

Relying on the tested maxim that nobody's stupider than an imperial soldier, you tilt the handlebars and twist the skimmer around. Its engines whine as the foils toss up a wall of water, marking your turn.

Now, heading back toward your startled pursuers, you try to figure the right curve between their zigzagging paths to make the two leaders turn toward each other and collide. You have to time this just right. Drawing a deep breath, you pull the skimmer's bubble hood down and scan the repeller readout.

Now! When the lead pair gets close enough to breathe on you, you jerk up on the handlebars and send the vehicle plunging beneath the surface. The water is clear and warm. Oxygen supplies kick in as the repeller field activates to keep water out of the hood. You look up and back, still holding your breath.

It works! The fast-moving water-sleds can't maneuver in time, and the two soldiers collide head-on. The skimmer foils break, the gyros go out, and two small craft spin away underwater, to disappear in glorious twin explosions. You start breathing again.

But four still pursue. No sense going back to the surface where they can surround you. With the remaining soldiers close behind, you head for the reef.

The clear, slightly bluish water of Pellaj surrounds your skimmer. Ahead, the coral reef looms like a city of columns and twisting tunnels.

You only wish you had time to observe the spectacular beauty of this alien reef. Bizarre corals twist in spirals and form netlike lattices; starlike creatures in a dozen colors crawl slowly from arch to arch; exotic underwater blooms wave in the surf; a fleeing pilot twists and turns through the columns.

That last is you, of course. In and out among the dark tunnels you try to shake off your pursuers. What creature may lurk in the next tunnel? You don't dare think. All you can do is hold tight to the handlebars.

Tilting their grips, you slide the skimmer down a dark tunnel in the reef. The dive brings you face-to-snout with three pairs of glittering eyes, more teeth than necessary, and a savage disposition. A moraylin, one of the most dangerous predators on any world.

Even the Domains are better than this, you think as you slam into full reverse. The bubble hood strikes the tunnel ceiling, the craft bounces, and you whisk out of the tunnel at an angle, right past two very startled Domain soldiers.

They can't stop in time. They jet right into the jaws of the monstrous moraylin. Its jaws crunch both skimmers at a gulp, producing a brilliant (and messy!) explosion and an awesome crater in the reef.

Two more pursuers down, two left as you leave the reef behind. Ahead, you see a pack of Cetapods. There's nothing to do but head for them.

Like a single ship among one-kilometer Morione Cruisers, your little skimmer speeds through the pack. Their enormous black bulks create shifting curtains of shadow in the bright water. The soldiers close in.

You're speeding through the pack in the direction opposite their movement, so that they appear to rush

at you head-on. You see eyes as big as living rooms, red clusters of tentacles above them, and up ahead, a cavernous mouth opening to feed.

Now the troopers are in blaster range. Energy bolts steam through the water past you, moving closer—a hit! The skimmer rocks beneath you, and your head bumps painfully against the bubble hood. Things look bad, and you're ready to say farewell to Zygash, when suddenly a brilliantly crazy idea hits you.

Before thinking it through (that's not your style), you swivel the handlebars and send your skimmer hurtling straight for the mouth of the Cetapod!

To the creature, you're hardly a morsel. Your craft plunges between triple rows of teeth and down the narrow throat. For a tense moment, the bubble looks ready to collapse under the strain. Then you wash into a foul-smelling stomach, along with lots of water.

You had time to see the Domain guards pull up short behind you. They're stupid, but not as stupid as me! you think triumphantly, then try to rephrase your thoughts. Meanwhile, you turn on the skimmer radio to hear the troopers' report. "He's dead," they tell their base commander. "Nobody could survive that." Great! As soon as they go away, you'll blast out of this red prison and—

Red. Say, how come it's light inside this stomach?

Someone taps on your bubble dome. Startled, you stare up to see a familiar—and friendly—face, and unlock the bubble dome.

Go to 6.

42

"You may depart," Jorth says, dismissing the soldiers. As they march out, he continues speaking. "I remain safe from your assault, Captain Hayl. You cannot consider harming me. Such action would only bring you into conflict with my new bodyguard." At his words, a tall figure steps from the shadows.

"Gash!" you cry. This is the worst shock yet. Seeing Zygash the G'rax holding a blaster rifle and standing guard over the repellent Baron Jorth—

Jorth chuckles. "Surprised, Hayl? Surprised that the Domain can reach out, across half the galaxy if need be, to shackle a single rebel with, if I may so phrase it, the bonds of loyalty?"

"That's not loyalty!" you shout back, gesturing at Gash. "That's brainwashing. It's—"

"It is the Subverter," says Jorth. "The mind weapon that will guarantee the Domain's supremacy. Think of it, Hayl: No one is safe. From its secret location in this system, the Subverter can find anyone's mind and mold it like putty, creating a willing servant—I shall not say 'slave,' out of respect for our scaly friend here—of the Domain."

Seeing Zygash's angry expression, you know Jorth's claims are true, and it scares you. You make a show of bravado, as much to bolster your own courage as anything. "You're through, Jorth! I'll sink this place from under you!"

Jorth laughs . . . and Zygash joins him. "Oh, Hayl, you are indeed amusing. Such sentiment was also expressed by the Cetapod Resistance leader. Now, of course, the beast is in my custody, to do with as I please. Much like yourself."

He continues, "You have played into my hands at every step. Once we obtained your G'rax friend, I knew it would be only a short while before you arrived as well."

"What do you want with us?"

"That I shall not tell you, Captain Hayl."

"Where's my ship?"

"The *Prosperogenesis*? Ah, your ship is most interesting from an engineering standpoint, I am told," says Jorth.

"Well, I try."

"Indeed. A robot pilot has flown it to the technical laboratories on the nearby asteroid mine of Dvaad, where technicians will disassemble it to discover the nature of your modifications. Then, of course, they will melt your ship to slag and discard it." He smiles.

"You melt my ship, and you'll join it in the slag heap, Jorth!"

His smile broadens. "I weary of this," says Jorth, though you see by his smug expression he's not at all weary of taunting you. "Now we shall begin our little diversion."

He pushes a button on the arm of his bodychair, and a wall slides back to reveal a balcony overlooking a lighted arena. The walls are white and smooth, the ceiling high, the floor featureless except for a few stains you easily identify.

With more button pushing, Jorth slides his bodychair onto the balcony, then sends a stairway descending to the floor below. Troopers arrive to wrestle you through the doorway and down onto the arena floor. Around and above, soldiers peer down at you. Their manner, like the light and the air, is cool. Escape looks hopeless.

"Hayl, you will enjoy hearing that I have been instructed not to harm you," Jorth calls from above. For a moment you wonder who instructed him, but his next words drive the thought from your mind. "However, harm is such a vague term. I interpret it to mean that you must not be killed. There is great latitude before that point, as my bodyguard will show."

Down the stairway comes Zygash, holding a blaster rifle. He looks grim and determined. Jorth smiles as he retracts the stairway, leaving you alone to face your closest friend in mortal combat.

"Wait!" you call nervously. "Jorth, we can negotiate—" Laughter bursts from the soldiers. "Well, maybe not. But—but this fight is rigged! Yeah, look, Gash's got a blaster, and I've got my bare hands. This won't be much of a show for you, Jorth, if I don't get a weapon of my own!" You hope he'll buy it. The odds may be hopeless, but you always feel better with a blaster in your hand.

"A weapon?" says Jorth. "But of course, Captain Hayl." Over the balcony railing falls a woven hyperlon net, followed by a dagger. "Net and sword, a time-honored tradition among gladiators," Jorth finishes, then laughs.

You barely have time to scoop up the net and blade before the G'rax rushes you. Do you have it in you to attack your best friend? You'd rather not find out, especially when you have nothing but a net and dagger against Zygash's blaster rifle.

You try reasoning with him, hoping to penetrate the Domain's mind-control. "Gash, it's me, I'm your friend. The Domain's making you do this—" It sounds weak even to your own ears, and you're hardly surprised when Zygash's scaly fist slams against your ear.

Well, at least he didn't fire his blaster, you think optimistically. Then Zygash fires his blaster. The bolt of energy barely misses your head.

If you fight Gash after all, go to 8.
If you keep trying to reason with him, go to 87.

43

The noise rises with every step down the corridor. Screams, crashes, explosions every moment, and growing under it all, the surge of onrushing water. For a tense moment you're afraid you won't get out before the entire city sinks, but then you emerge at the source of the sound: a ferrocrete canopy extending down into the sea, a "wharf" for water landings.

Sea-skimmers are all around, as well as larger seacraft that you couldn't pilot alone. The entire canopy is rippling like a canvas tarpaulin, and tremendous waves are washing up almost to your feet. You'd better grab a skimmer before there's nowhere left to stand.

As you start to choose one, a blow from behind sends you toppling to the deck. Zygash has awakened, and he attacks you!

With the *Ocean Lord* sinking under your feet and the seas of Pellaj licking at the guardrails, you attack your best friend.

You keep telling yourself, It's for the Resistance. For the Resistance, you dodge Gash's lethal, swinging left hooks and kick him in his soft, tender spot under the floating ribs. For the Resistance, you duck his combination left, right-high, right-low combination punches (how often did he try that on you when you sparred together as kids?), and you drive a fist into the soft spot under his chin. You know all his moves, all his weak points, and you exploit them ruthlessly—for the Resistance.

After a few moments of this, you hate the Resistance, and yourself.

Zygash falls to the deck, badly hurt. Green blood mingles with seawater on his purple scales. You stand over him, tears in your eyes, mustering the courage to do something awful—

No, it's crazy, you can't do it. You turn away.

Behind you, Gash roars. You brace for the attack, resolved not to fight him again. But then you realize what he said, and turn around in astonishment.

"Gash—you're okay? Did I—are you—is it true?"

The G'rax leaps up and sweeps his arms around you, not in an attack but in a tremendous hug. "*Gnnnuuurrnnh vrruuungh hnnnaaargh, hnnnrrgh!*" he cries, and you have to agree.

But there's no time for an emotional reunion. Now that the shock of approaching death has snapped Gash out of the Domain's mind control, you have to get away before the stronghold sinks from under you!

Go to 74.

44

You need to take out this guard, but you can't use a blaster or you'll alert the whole stronghold. And there's that surveillance camera too. Well, the Domain's greatest weakness is that its servants are corrupt.

You approach the sentry casually. "Trooper Karo Geenan? I have your high sky winnings, over 500 debits."

"I'm not—"

"My buddy Dobbo sent me. Told me to have you count it, all 520 DMs. Said you'd give me 10 as a tip."

"My name isn't—I don't—" The soldier pauses. "500?" he asks.

"And 20. Dobbo said I'd get 10, or maybe 15, if you want."

The soldier is silent for long moments. "All right, give it to me," he says, holding out his gloved hand.

You smirk and cast an eye at the camera. "Not in front of company."

He follows your glance, pauses again, then pulls out a comm unit. "Nexus, Sentry 1245 here," he says.

"Who's there?"

"1245 acknowledged. Glennet here."

"Hi, Glen, it's Murko," says the sentry. Belatedly he catches himself and looks at you. "I, uh, I use 'Murko' as a code name." You nod understandingly.

Murko asks for a "test" of the surveillance camera. The chuckle at the other end shows that Glennet isn't fooled, but the indicator light on the camera blinks out.

"Okay, let me have it," says Murko, and you let him have it—a stun-bolt from your blaster, square on his chest!

You holster your pistol and pull the unconscious guard into the room before the camera comes back on. You hope you'll have time to look around in there before his absence raises the alarm. You signal Wrench, and the little maintenance bot wheels into the room after you.

The room inside is a huge chamber lined with complicated machinery, catwalks, and gantryways. It's lit by a ring of white panels surrounding the ceiling. But for all the bright light, the shadows cast by the many tanks of liquid make the room a dark, brooding, gloomy place. Noises drown the liquid's quiet bubbling: the steady beeping of machinery, the rumbling moan of an immense Cetapod trapped in the largest tank, and the low growl of a G'rax.

In front of the giant Cetapod's tank you see one Domain soldier—and Zygash beside him, carrying a Domain blaster rifle. Gash looks just as he always did, a scaly purple giant with four huge arms and a wide mouth full of sharp teeth. So your mind turns to thoughts of diverting Gash and the guard from their post.

Your best bet is a blaster shot against the far wall, to produce a nice explosion that will draw away Zygash and the guard. You brace against a fluid canister and take careful aim.

Spang! Sparks fly and pipes hiss. G'rax and trooper run to investigate, beyond a bank of machinery. You take half a moment to admire the nice results of your shot. Must have hit a circulation pipe, you think. Not bad! Then you rush for the tank.

The Cetapod rumbles in surprise as you approach. The creature is so big it's best not to think about it. A quick once-over shows that if you trigger the razor switches on the tank controls, the tank bottom will open to the deep ocean beneath and the Cetapod can swim free. But that's bound to make a lot of noise; if you let the creature loose, you'll probably be discovered.

With your translation device, you can at least talk with the Cetapod and get an idea what to do next. You steal up beside the huge tank and speak quietly into the mouthpiece of your harness. But your volume level means nothing to the translator. It still turns your words into full-blown Cetapod speech, and that's loud enough to drown out a launch siren!

The deafening moans from your chest harness alert Zygash and the guard instantly. They run toward the tank.

You don't see any way around it. For his own good, you must fire a well-placed stun shot, dropping Zygash where he stands. Seeing his still, unconscious form, you wonder what else you may have to do on this mission.

The first thing is to fire at the other guard, who was alerted by your blaster shot. Now you give him plenty more shots, but instead of alerting him further, they send him into oblivion.

Now, at last, you can use the translator. More a subsonic vibration than a sound, the Cetapod's voice is so deep you can hardly hear it, but so loud it's deafening. The Resistance device turns the creature's

words into cultured human speech and plays it in your ear.

"This one is grateful Haurrassith, tiny swimmer in the great world. This one, angry Haurrassith, swam to free this one's people from the tiny killers above the world." (The creature must be talking about the Domain's "fishing expeditions" against the gentle Cetapods.)

"How were you caught?" you ask. The machine's speaker bellows and roars. Haurrassith's tremendous eye blinks in comprehension.

"This one, mournful Haurrassith, placed a shiny-hot-net, given by the good tiny ones, under this place to put the killers out of the world. But before slow Haurrassith could bring the shiny-hot-net to make sun beneath this place, this one was taken from the great world to this place by the tiny bad killers."

Caught while setting a Resistance explosive. "Is the melter-net—the shiny-hot-web—still beneath the city? Does the Domain know it's there?"

"Shiny-hot-web still waits in the great world. No eye has seen it, no ear heard it, but this one's, eager Haurrassith's. Free this one, tiny thing, to swim again in the world and make the sun beneath this place."

Sounds good. You flip the switches that pull back the tank bottom, and the creature drops away into the seas of Pellaj like a spaceliner moving out of dry dock.

Move fast, because you haven't got much time before Haurrassith sets that melter and dissolves the entire substructure of the *Ocean Lord*. You have to get Zygash back to the Resistance so the medics there can cure his brainwashing.

Go to 63.

45

In choosing how to leave Silverlight, you return to the *Genesis*'s old hangar bay to review your few options. Wrench, the MRP maintenance robot, is still cleaning up. "Welcome back, sir," it says. "I am proud to have you as my new owner."

"Huh?"

"When the G'rax pilot blasted off without warning, your ship did great damage to the equipment around—not including me, happily. So the spaceport has collected the insurance bond you posted and written off the equipment here—including me. You own me, and all of this, now." One pincered hand gestures at the heaps of twisted wreckage waiting by the disposal chute.

You look at the junk and groan, then look at the

small square robot and groan twice. "One more mouth to feed," you say.

"Please take me with you on your perilous mission to clear Master Zygash, sir. I would feel honored to help you. Or, if you fail, think how comforting it will be, as you die, to know I will be nearby to clean up the mess."

"I feel better already. Okay, Wrench, you're in."

"Very good, Captain Hayl. You will need transport off-planet. I know of a Resistance ship available in hangar bay 88, although it is rather old. Also, you may have heard that a miner named Jaspon Dentoze is seeking companionship on a journey to the Dvaad asteroid system. Then, of course, there are commercial flights to Pellaj on luxury ships—I've always wanted to see those huge liners, Captain."

"Spaceliners?" You snort. "I've flown half the sectors in the Domain. I don't go tourist class, okay?"

"They're wonderful ships, sir. You can check me as baggage, by the way. Not that I'm dropping a hint or anything."

How will you leave Silverlight?

If you take a commercial spaceliner to Pellaj, like a common tourist, go to 56.

If you go with the miner Jaspon Dentoze to Dvaad, go to 37.

If you want to look at or take the Resistance ship, go to 40.

46

"Sorry," you tell Jaspon, "it's your statue. Use your own shirt."

He stares in disbelief. "You won't do one small favor to repair this colossal work of art? You, a passenger on my ship? That's my life! It's happening all over again! Slave over a creative effort, and some ignorant space-jockey decides *he knows better*! He *decides how it comes out*! Yaaahh, I won't take this anymore!"

"Wait!" His arms are flying wildly, dangerously near the ship's controls. "Okay, Jaspon, calm down. I'll give you my shirt."

After all, why not? Once you see a gigantic statue of a miner, hanging in deep space and made entirely of shirts, other concerns seem trivial. You peel off your shirt and hand it to Dentoze.

"Thank you," he says. "Now if you will be good enough to don the lifesuit in yonder locker, I shall supervise your repair of the sculpture."

"What?"

"Fear not, the suit expands or shrinks to fit the wearer. The attached jet-pack furnishes mobility. I, the artist, must look on from a distance to ensure that symmetry is maintained."

You examine the locker, the lifesuit, the pack, and your own options. Nothing looks promising, and so, minutes later, you emerge from the *Small Waist*'s airlock.

The sleek lifesuit clings to your body, reflecting the blackness of space. The jet-pack carries you to the floating fabric sculpture of Jaspon Dentoze. Big as a hangar building, the frame is made of wire fine enough to slice through the suit. With exquisite care, you tie your shirt onto the giant nose.

When you float back to the mine ship, your jet-pack is almost exhausted. You knock on the airlock door. "Okay, Jaspon, I'm done," you tell him over the suit radio. "You can let me in now. Hurry—my nose itches, and I can't scratch it through the helmet."

"Fine job, Hayl! The profile is perfect now. How do you like it?" Jaspon's voice is a purr over the radio.

"I like it a whole bunch. Let me in."

"You sound insincere."

"No, really, a lovely job. A lovely work of art, I mean. It's just, uh, lovely." You fight to keep fear out of your voice.

"Hayl, I am not one to harbor hypocrites. I detest hypocrites! I shall not grant them the attentions of my companionship. I shall return to eDrive soon. Perhaps solitary contemplation of my likeness will enrich you. Good-bye."

Blast it, why did you know this was going to happen? What will you do?

If you try to sabotage the ship, preventing the jump to eDrive, go to 7.

If you try bribing Jaspon, go to 57.

If you try to get Wrench the maintenance robot to help you, go to 53.

47

"Not to worry," you tell the guard, passing the room. You walk rapidly down the hallway surrounding this large room. There appears to be no other entrance. You notice one small ventilation hatch high up on a wall.

"Wrench, wait here," you tell the robot. "When you hear me shout for you, go back to the entrance we passed and get into the room."

"You're going into great danger, Captain Hayl," says Wrench calmly. "Would it count as a shout to me if you're screaming in agony?"

You almost think this over. "Never mind, don't think about it," you tell the bot. Then, floating upward with no more than a slight whine from the antigrav belt, you pry away a vent grate and enter the chamber.

You're in a webwork of catwalks and gantryways near the ceiling of an enormous room. The gloomy place is crowded with torture tanks of bubbling fluid, with machinery on all the walls and in every corner.

Noises of pain rise from the tank below you, where a huge Cetapod lies trapped. Terrible-smelling vapors waft up to you from the bubbling tank.

Below you, guarding the Cetapod's tank, stands a Domain soldier—and Zygash, the G'rax, carrying a Domain blaster rifle. Your friend stands easily, looking almost bored.

Crouching on the walkway, behind a bank of fluid canisters, you decide to wait for the soldier to leave. What if Gash leaves first? Worries and questions fill your mind, but after a short while, the soldier signals that he's taking a break, and goes out of sight past a bank of machinery. Gash is alone in the torture chamber.

You want to call out to him, but something about Gash makes you uneasy. Best not to take anything for granted in this strange situation. You tense to begin a stealthy approach toward Zygash. You're almost ready—

"This area off limits to all personnel," says a mechanical voice.

Startled, you turn. A maintenance robot trundles toward you along the catwalk. "Shhh!" you hiss.

"You will have to leave immediately," it says, none too quietly. Gash hasn't noticed it yet, but if there's much more talk . . .

You plant a hand over the bot's speaker and push. "Mnnff?" the unbalanced mechanical says, surprised. It flops backward on the catwalk, arms and extensors flaying.

As you grope for its off switch, one of those arms accidentally strikes you across the chest, knocking the wind from you. You're sent sailing into the air over the open torture tank. The robot makes no sound; maybe it's speechless with surprise.

One more smooth move by the idol of the Resistance, you think. You activate the antigrav harness and fly silently over the torture tank below. Holding your breath against its foul vapors, you fly low over the imprisoned Cetapod like a skimmer over smooth terrain. Crossing the tail, you sail across the streamlined body for a count of twenty, finally passing between the twin clumps of manipulatory tentacles above the creature's eyes. Incredible that a living being could grow this large, and feel so much pain.

You twist in the air and land to one side of the tank, out of sight. Edging around a bank of fluid canisters, you see Zygash alone.

Nearby you notice the tank controls. A quick examination tells you that simply throwing a row of switches will retract the tank bottom, allowing the captive Cetapod to swim down into the ocean beneath the stronghold. But the noise would probably give away your position.

The idea strikes at once. You peel off the antigrav harness and strap it onto—well, what have you got? A small fluid canister will do. Then you send it floating silently, tumbling end over end across the chamber toward the far corner. There, you figure, the thing should bump around enough to lure Zygash out of earshot.

You didn't figure, though, that the Cetapod in the tank would be so famished that it will snag anything that moves. As the belt flies over the open tank, a red tentacle lashes out and dexterously wraps around the harness. The Cetapod, starved from its long imprisonment, pulls the belt down to its huge mouth and swallows it!

Blast! You let out a groan—and that's all Zygash needs to spot you. You hold your breath, hoping he's just been pretending. But Gash roars for help, then growls an order to drop your weapon. Zygash, your best friend, looks as hostile as the soldier who comes to back him up.

This, more than anything, makes you give up hope. Hands on your head, you rise.

And so does the Cetapod.

At first you don't notice, because the soldier is frisking you. It pains you to see Gash growling instructions to the guard, just like a Domain trooper. The G'rax recognizes you, but he doesn't enjoy seeing you at all.

You look away from him, just in time to see the colossal Cetapod float higher in the torture tank—higher—and then out of the water, like a Morione Cruiser leaving port. The belt, you think as your eyes bulge. The belt is still working!

"Come on," says the soldier, while the Cetapod floats silently in your direction. "We're taking you to Jorth. You'll be a big surprise to drop on him."

The soldier sees you staring upward, follows your gaze, and a very, very big surprise drops on him. You feel a rush of air and smell a moist, sour smell, and then a flanged tail larger than a ship bulkhead sweeps down, driving the trooper against the far wall. His armor cracks when he hits. Sliding down, he falls still.

You see nothing but a black, barnacle-encrusted expanse of flesh. The creature turns ponderously, floating high above the floor. For a moment, one gigantic eye, uncannily humanoid, regards you. You know that absolutely nothing can protect you. Then its tail lashes out again—against the near wall. The wall collapses, alarms sound, and the Cetapod pulls itself out of the chamber with its twin clusters of tentacles.

Zygash is sprawled on the floor, apparently alive after a glancing blow from the Cetapod's tail. You rush to look. Yes, he'll be fine. But how will you get him out before the Domains arrive? He's way too heavy for you to carry. . . .

Crash! Brrrak-k-koooommmm!

No he's not, you decide as the explosions start nearby. Grunting with effort, you hoist Gash on your shoulders. It's amazing how pressure has increased your strength. You'll have to remember that for future reference: All it takes is a revenge-crazed flying whale trying to destroy the city.

That's what you see as you struggle into the corridor. The windows are smashed. The ceiling is gone. Walls, panels, struts, and support beams have vanished in a straight line that leads toward the center of the *Ocean Lord*. Technicians and guards and bureaucrats rush around in the wreckage. Alarms blare, evacuation notices repeat every ten seconds, and high winds whistle through the corridors. Above it all you hear the rumbling roar of the Cetapod.

"Wrench!"

"Here, Captain Hayl!" In the confusion you don't spot the boxy maintenance bot until it wheels up to you. "Ah, you've found Master Zygash, sir! Good work. It's too bad you and he are likely to drown when this city sinks."

"Make yourself useful and carry Gash." You unload the G'rax into Wrench's metal arms, and together you rush for the spaceport.

But first you arrive at an atrium. Here you stop in your tracks.

The Cetapod is here, causing havoc beyond your imagination. Floating nose down as if diving, the creature fills the entire atrium from ceiling skylight to polished floor. Its tentacles rip antigrav elevators from their tracks and send them buzzing toward offices. Its tail sweeps forward, crashing through a line of support pillars—then back, removing a squad

of Elite Imperial Soldiers on the return stroke. Choking dust saturates the air.

No weapon does more than scorch the Cetapod's hide. The stronghold's heavy weaponry, fixed on the hull, protects only from sea and airborne assaults. No one planned for this!

Amid the cracks and crashes, a deeper crack overhead warns you to get away fast. Far down in the bass register, the cracking grows louder. As you escape down a corridor, the entire ceiling caves in on the Cetapod. But its tail sends debris flying. Chunks of ferrocrete as big as houses punch through walls, starting fountains of sparks. Twisting once, twice, the furious Cetapod swims high in the air, free of the wreckage, then dives through the riddled wall to inflict still more destruction.

You watch as it disappears. "Talk about the big one that got away," you murmur reverently. You hurry on.

Alarms whoop as survivors crowd the corridors. You've gotten turned around in the confusion. Smoke fills the hallway, obscuring direction signs. Everyone around is too panicky to answer questions. One corridor, crowded with people, slopes gently downward. Over it you see a sign reading TO WHARF. You think, Well, that will work. "Come on, Wrench! We're finding a skimmer!" You run down the corridor, the shouts of the mob loud in your ears.

Go to 43.

48

"Carabajal's just using you for his own ends," you tell the Kakklakks. "You mean nothing to him. The

Domain is evil! It's brought nothing but misery to ten thousand worlds, and this one is no different. Don't you want freedom, for others as well as yourself? Don't you want to destroy something that grinds down a thousand intelligent races?"

Oh, yes, intelligence, says the hive-mind. We know of that. We have no use for it, and no cares for otherbeings who indulge in it.

"What? You're intelligent yourselves."

Separate, we are simply alive. We come together only when necessary to deal with invaders like this humanbeing. Living and intelligence have little to do with one another.

"Hey, it's done all right by us. We've spread to most of the planets in the galaxy."

The Kakklakks pulse more erratically—laughter? *Yes, the humanbeing is proud of its intelligence. But intellect means division, faction, struggle. What the Dukebeing calls "wars." Wars—inevitable, destructive. We are Kakklakks. We will continue. But in a thousand of the humanbeing's lifetimes, perhaps less, its race will be gone, its struggles merely stories told to entertain and educate beings far away.*

"Is that so? Well, I intend to see that this story has a happy ending. Where's the door?" Furious and frustrated, you look for the tunnel exit.

The Subverter ignores you. *This "freedom," this "evil," these are curious notions. By knowing such, we improve dealings with the Dukebeing and others of its kind. The humanbeing must merge its mind with ours.* The pile of Kakklakks creatures dissolves as individual natives leap down and reform the pile around your feet—your legs—your waist. . . .

In a few moments the Kakklakks will bury you completely. You have no idea what will happen then, but you don't like it at all so far. But your struggle is, at most, a minor inconvenience to the Kakklakks. Bodies weigh down your arms, mandibles and legs hold your own legs fast. All you manage to do is fall to the ground, crushing a few natives beneath you.

One of the surviving insects—and there are many—crawls across your chest and rests on your face. The process of merging begins.

A Kakklakk opens its mouth and spits a thick gelatin of some kind over your face. It crawls up your chest and inserts two thin legs up your nostrils, through the gel. You gag by reflex, but find you can still breathe normally. Is the creature supplying you with air?

Insectlike natives crawl over you, front, back, and sides. They link up, legs to shell-ridges, and you're surrounded by a living net of alien flesh. In your mind you feel a new presence, and your life's memory flashes at inhuman speed across your awareness. The Subverter is ransacking your brain!

All at once you can breathe normally. The hive-mind frees you from its too-intimate touch. The Subverter's voice in your mind sounds amazed. *Ship! Humanbeing ship can carry us into the sky, find other colonies, breed!*

Its surprise quickly turns to fury. *Dukebeing did not correctly tell us concept of ship. Dukebeing kept us from going on to the destiny! No meeting—no young— chachukka kachakkack kalachachuk*—Its tirade reverts to a stream of its native sounds, less than a language but more than noise. Whatever it means, it sounds angry.

The individual Kakklakks leap from the pile. The insectile things swarm up the nearest tunnel, heading for the Domain mines. Furious clacking echoes down the tunnel and from other tunnels around. Telepathy, or instinctive signals? It sounds like the whole Kakklakk population is on the warpath.

You follow slowly, dreading what you'll see. Human shouts signal the start of the disaster, and alarms of all kinds follow quickly. Sirens drown out the Kakklakk cries, but occasional explosions tell you a battle is raging.

You feel sure the Kakklakks can't possibly stand against the Domain's weaponry: battalions of Elite Imperial Soldiers, blaster weapons, cruisers, chemical weapons. . . . Against these, the Kakklakks have only surprise and a ruthless fury.

Nearing the mine complex, you find that this was enough. Parts of the tunnel are rimed with frost, but others are sweltering; Kakklakks must have gotten into the life support system. Robots are systematically tearing their surroundings to pieces; Kakklakks had gotten into the robot control center. Tunnels are collapsing; deep in the mines, Kakklakks had found explosives. Bodies, human and Kakklakk, lie everywhere.

Where are the soldiers? You hear no blaster fire. You learn the answer when you happen on a barracks littered with armored bodies. Of course—with the power to control minds, the Subverter need only reform, force one poor victim to open fire on his fellows, and the resulting firefight takes out everyone.

Selective control must have neutralized the whole colony in moments. You wander through the devastated base for a long time. Except for a lucky accident, this would have been the Resistance.

The Subverter finds you before you find it. The reins of control tighten on your mind, leading you to the laboratories. No one survives here. Techs armed with chemical tanks lie in the tunnel. The Kakklakks must have attacked them before they could spray the chemical.

The call comes from an underground hangar not far from the technical labs. The *Prosperogenesis* sits here, dismantled, covered with more Kakklakks than you realized lived on Dvaad. Hundreds and hundreds of insects crawl over the ship, carrying parts of your beloved vessel out the exit and up a tunnel. The Subverter hive-mind directs them from its station beneath the main hull.

"Hey—hey! What's this?" you cry.

Amid the chaos a maintenance robot spots you and wheels over. "Captain Hayl, you're back!" Wrench observes. "I've found your ship, but it seems a lot of insect natives have too."

"Not now, Wrench. What's going on, Subverter?"

Ship, the Subverter explains. *We learned of it in the humanbeing's mind. We must take it to the surface of the world, and the humanbeing will take us to other colonies.*

"Uhhh. . . ." This is a lot to grapple with. And it gets stranger yet.

Go to 36.

49

You pull out the portable holo-viewer and the tapes. "Do you follow sports?" you ask. No reply. "No, I didn't think so. Let me show you some of the great entertainment you can get by joining the Resistance."

You pop in a tape and activate the viewer. Two teams of miniature figures float before you, engaged in their contest over possession of the energy-globe that means victory. "See those guns that propel the ball around the arena? These guys are the best in the galaxy at that. Look here, that guy who's floating forward, he's the squad topper. His team gets points when he holds the ball. Great match, huh?"

The Subverter says nothing for a long time. It finally asks, *This is being produced by that device?*

"Huh? Yeah." You explain recordings to the hive-mind.

And these humanbeings strive for supremacy in this field?

"Yeah." You explain competitions to the hive-mind. It understands the concept immediately.

Does winner eat loser?

You realize that if you try to explain everything that citizens of the galaxy take for granted about gravball, you'll die of old age. "No," you say. "Just watch, okay?"

It watches in silence. You can't tell how this is going over, but it hasn't tried to eat you yet. After a time the Subverter grunts as one team's squad topper scores a goal. A few moments later the opponents narrowly miss a goal themselves, and in your mind the Subverter says, *Very close.*

You move slowly away from the holo-viewer. The Subverter pays no attention. The alien hive-mind appears engrossed in the galactic quarter-finals of the most recent Interplanetary Gravball League tournament. If only the promoters could see this, you think. So what if the Resistance hangs in the balance? Why not take a break? Kick back with the Domain's new super-weapon and enjoy a good gravball game!

You wouldn't have thought you could relax here. But as the tournament continues, and the hive-mind remains absorbed in it, you stretch out by a cattle-bug for some rest. Odd how a sportscast can make even this alien asteroid cavern seem as pale and routine as your sleeping bay on the *Genesis*.

The Subverter's mental shout awakens you. *Humanbeing! Does it have any more of these struggles for supremacy?*

"Uh, no. But you liked them, right?"

Most interesting. We will request the Dukebeing to provide more. We do not believe the humanbeing's Resistance is the only source for these contests.

Oh, well. At least it seems better disposed toward

you. You put one of the programs back on. Leaving the Subverter fascinated by the rerun, you escape down a tunnel and make your way to the human area of the colony.

It's a relief to see other human beings, and even robots, when you reach the mining operation. The clanking gravsleds on their rails overhead, the towers of administrative offices in their caverns, the loader-bots and technicians all going about their duties—after the Subverter, it's practically home sweet home!

You don't forget for a moment that you're looking for your ship. From long experience, you have a fair idea where the hangar bays must lie. You go down the tunnels and are surprised to find that the complex takes on a new character, that of a technical laboratory. The robots are lab types, and the maintenance bots look shinier.

Then you find an underground hangar. And inside, totally dismantled and useless, is the *Prosperogenesis*.

Your ship is a hulk. Spread around the disassembled shell are the pipes, braces, circuits, panels, computers, stabilizers, and wingnuts that you lovingly assembled into that wonderful vehicle. The Domain obviously wanted to see how you did it.

"Oh, baby," you say to yourself, over and over, fighting back tears. The parts are spread out across the hangar floor, sorted by type and size. You wander among them hopelessly.

"Captain Hayl!" Wrench the robot wheels up from a corridor. "I've been looking for you. The Domain has dismantled your ship."

You have no energy even for a wisecrack. "I know," you sigh.

Humanbeing! you hear in your mind, and you turn. There in the doorway writhes a pile of Kakklakks, the Subverter hive-mind. *We find interest in the contests of supremacy the humanbeing provides. We desire more.*

"Tough. I haven't got any." You look around. "I haven't got anything left."

"Who are you talking to, Captain Hayl?" asks Wrench.

"It takes too long to explain, Wrench. Quiet, okay?"

The faceted eyes take in the entire hangar and all the parts of your ship. *What is this device?*

"It doesn't show holo-tapes, if that's what you want. It's my ship. Your buddies have taken it apart. Now I'll never get off this lousy world!"

Clarify. This is a means of transport? It carries human-beings into the sky? This is ship?

"Right three times."

Will ship carry us into the sky? To other worlds, to find other colonies and breed?

You pause, turning this idea over. But why lead the thing on? You can't fly now, so why fool it? "It would, except it's broken. Dismantled. Taken apart into component pieces. Nonfunctional." Your voice breaks and you stop.

We did not fully understand the concept of ship. Ship was not correctly relayed to us by the Dukebeing. We will render the ship functional, and you will take us to other colonies.

That's when strange things start happening.

Go to 36.

50

Jorth is probably too terrified to lie right now. So, though Gash grumbles suspiciously, you let the Domain governor lead you across the shaking space-port. He waddles surprisingly fast for his considerable weight, but because you're clutching his collar, you have no trouble keeping up. You wonder, though, at those odd bulges around his knees and elbows. Hidden weapons?

You haul him up short, but he points ahead. "There she is!" Before you is a luxury starcruiser, shiny and powerful, with multiple ion engines in a swept-back design. It's so well stabilized that it seems to float unaffected above the rocking launch platform.

Jorth stumbles up the closed gangway and punches a quick security code. You tense—an alarm?—but the door slides down, and no battalions of soldiers rush out. You, Gash, and Wrench follow the governor aboard. "Stay back here and watch our hostage, Gash," you order as you head for the yacht's cockpit.

You whistle at the frills this beauty offers. The launch sequence moves along like a dream. Your blastoff is smooth and effortless. As the stronghold cracks up beneath you, you think, Finally, I get to leave a place in style!

Go to 71.

51

By reflex you raise your blaster; you have time for a clear shot at Zygash. Then you look at your hand like it belongs to someone else, and pull it down again.

You try to reason with the G'rax, appealing to his spirit of friendship. "Gash, I can't fight you. You're family."

Zygash creeps toward you behind a line of low crates. "*Hnnrraaaarrnghhh*," Zygash says.

You sigh. "No, I won't surrender. I don't know what they did to you, Gash, but I want to get my hands on whoever did it."

Gash's rifle pokes up over a crate and fires. The shot goes wild, and the G'rax seems slower than you remember. Whether or not this comes of his brain-washing, you have time to sight his rifle and blast the weapon out of his hands. You rush out and point your blaster. Gash stands and raises all four arms.

"Okay, now, it's me, Rogan," you say as you approach the G'rax. "C'mon, buddy, whatever they did to you, you have to—"

With amazing speed the scaly giant pulls back both right arms and strikes you. You reel back and fall heavily. He hit you! You hate to think you could actually fire on your best friend.

More desperate now, you raise your voice. "Gash, I don't want to hurt you! Remember me? Whatever they did to you, it's not as strong as what we have." But your words mean nothing to the enraged G'rax. He strikes at you again, and it feels like the blow cracks a rib.

Stunned by Gash's ferocious attack, you fall to the ground. Got to get up, got to—you're helpless. You can't move, though your life literally depends on it. Through bleary eyes you see Zygash, your best friend, standing over you. He's ready to strike the killing blow.

Your lips are bruised, your throat tight. You can hardly say the word: "Gash. . . ." Probably your last word, you think as the G'rax growls. You suppose it's fitting that this supposed rescue mission ends with its target's name on your lips.

The rifle's stock rises, rises. In a moment it will come down. In a moment your life will end.

In that moment, Zygash pauses. He shivers from head to foot, and seems almost ready to fall. Then, with a howl of anguish, he hurls the weapon aside and scoops you up. "*Hnnnaaaarraagha!*" he shouts.

"Gash! You're back, you're back!" You're babbling, overcome with joy and relief. The G'rax has thrown off the chains that held his mind.

Once you're on your feet, you realize how many questions you have. "What happened to you? How did you get here? Are you all right?" And so on, as though you'd been bursting with them and never realized it.

"*Nnnnhrrahaaagh vrrrng hnnrrraaar,*" the G'rax tells you.

"I knew it! That's what I told everyone. But—why is the Cetapod here?"

"*Vnnnrrhhgh hraaahn hnnnaaargh. Vrunnh.*"

"Oh, brother. What was it, a melter-net?" Gash nods. "Right. Well, then let's let him free so he can finish arming it, shall we?" You throw the razor switches that open the torture tank. With an expression in its eye that may be gratitude, the Resistance leader on Pellaj sinks into the ocean beneath the stronghold to finish the work that brought about its capture.

"Okay, we haven't got much time before this place blows." You and Gash rush out into the hallway, ignoring the calls of guards, ignoring the alarm, heading for the spaceship docking yard. Guards chase you in ones and twos, and then in squads. Blast doors slide shut just moments after you skirt past them. The Domain closes in.

Then, when capture seems inevitable, a tremendous explosion rocks the stronghold. "There goes the net!" you shout to Gash, and he growls triumphantly. The floor tilts as the *Ocean Lord*'s substructure melts away in terrific heat. The stronghold immediately starts to sink. In the chaos that follows, you easily escape the soldiers.

Gash guides you to the landing field and docking yard. There you find an array of spacecraft, rocking gently with the tremors of the sinking city. Which one?

Gash gestures: "*Rrrauuughaaahnnng!*" Sure enough, it is! Baron Jorth's own luxury yacht sits on the deck nearby, apparently ready to launch.

"A slime like Jorth must be ready for a hasty exit all the time," you tell Gash as he blasts open the gangway lock. The ship's security alarm is lost in the clamor of alarms from a whole city. As the shipyard slips down toward the water, you rev the engines and blast away from the sinking *Ocean Lord*.

Gash howls a traditional G'rax chant of triumph, and you feel like joining him. Instead, you just laugh. "That's what I call going in style!"

Go to 71.

52

"Password?" you ask the soldier. "What's this about passwords? Jorth suspended them. You should have been informed at the briefing. Sayyy," you say suspiciously, "how come you didn't know that? What's your name, soldier?"

"I didn't hear anything about passwords being suspended."

"I asked your name, soldier!"

"Murko—sir."

"Murko, if I have to report back to Jorth that I couldn't secure the material he desires because you wouldn't let me in, what happens to your career?"

Well, it could be worse, you decide a few moments later. You're getting into the room, even if Murko the soldier has decided to accompany you.

The door slides back, and you enter a chamber bigger than a ship hangar bay. Lighted by panels near the high ceiling, the chamber is still gloomy. Catwalks line the walls like webs. Clear tanks filled with bubbling liquid cast shadows on corners cluttered with equipment. In a tank that could hold two dozen G12 Marauder XX ships floats one Cetapod, with no room to move. Its streamlined body and twin clusters of tentacles tremble with pain.

Murko leads you to two other soldiers guarding the Cetapod's tank. As you approach, you see a smaller tank beside it. In the smaller tank floats Zygash. All his arms hang loosely in the torture fluid, and he moans in pain. He must have been imprisoned when you broke the Subverter's control!

Your eyes widen, but you manage to keep calm as Murko leads you to the other two guards. You tell Murko, "That'll be all, soldier. Return to your post." After a moment of indecision, during which time you age about six months, Murko turns and goes back to his post. The door closes, leaving you alone with the two puzzled guards.

You try to bluff your way through: "Uh—tank inspector! Heard you have a lot of, um, aquarian feedback here. What do you know about it?"

Even though their visors conceal their expressions, you can tell they're not buying it. You wouldn't yourself.

"Well, if you don't know anything," you say smoothly, "I'll have to go back to the Central Office and check out the snafu." You turn away. Sometimes a show of nerve can get you out of a tight scrape.

This time it doesn't. You hear them readying their blaster rifles, so you spin, beating them to the draw. The day you can't out-draw a couple of Elite Imperials—well, that day has happened many times, frankly. But the past doesn't matter today. You fire—not at the two soldiers, but at a bank of containers behind them. If those labels are right . . .

Fwsssshhh! Yes! Streams of pressurized macracetylene gas jet out, crystallizing in the air as they hit the guards. Their blaster shots go wild as the gas blows them off balance, and then it's just one-two, and one-two more for good measure, to drop the guards with well-placed bolts.

You stare down at the unconscious soldiers and wipe moisture from your forehead. "Guess I was nervous," you tell Zygash. The G'rax pounds joyfully on the plastoid walls of the tank.

"There's something I've forgotten," you murmur to yourself. Just then the door to the chamber slides back, and Murko enters to investigate the commotion. He sees you, raises his rifle—and falls, dropped by your unerring blaster shot.

"Yeah, I knew something had slipped my mind." You check your blaster's power supply. Amazing that you have so many shots left! "Sometimes I surprise even myself," you say, then blow across the muzzle for luck.

"Hrrrrraaaannnngghaaa!"

"Right. Move back from this wall." You blast away at the wall, and in a flood of liquid Gash washes free

of the tank. Wet, smelly, and exhilarated, the giant
G'rax sweeps to his feet and grabs you in a suffocat-
ing hug. "Easy, Gash, easmmmph! Mmm gld
tsuhyuhtuh! Mmmph!"

You survive the reunion in only slightly worse
shape than you survived the blaster battle. With Gash
at your side at last, you decide what to do with the
captive Cetapod, who looks on from the other torture
tank. Then you remember: You carry a Cetapod translation device.

Go to 68 to use it.

53

You know the standard wavelength robots use to
talk among themselves. You shift your suit radio to
that frequency and hail Wrench. "Yes?" the robot
responds calmly.

"Wrench!" You fight to calm down. "Say, Wrench,
what about getting me back into the ship, okay?"

"I'd like to, Captain Hayl, but I'm sure this pilot
would restrain me before I can do so. I believe that if
it's left up to my efforts, you're going to freeze in the
depths of space."

"Uh-huh." Think, think. "Can Jaspon hear this conversation?"

"No, sir. It's internal."

"Okay, try this." You outline your plan. In
moments, you hear Wrench talking to Jaspon. "Look,
sir, Captain Hayl is trying to wreck your statue!"

"Where? Where is he? I don't see him!"

"I see him with my, um, hyperthermal sensors.
There, over the left shoulder! Fire, sir!"

The ship's little gun pod fires, hitting the statue.
"No, sir, you missed! Now he's jetting toward the

hip!" The beam fires again, and now the wire frame is starting to sag. A few more "sightings," a few shots, and the entire sculpture is a shapeless heap of fabric and wire.

Wrench opens the airlock door. "You may come in now, sir."

"Where's Jaspon?"

"He collapsed when the statue did, sir."

Jaspon is crushed. He puts up no resistance as you take the ship into eDrive and continue to Dvaad. You drop him off at a miners' aid station, where you hope they'll be able to console the aggrieved artist.

Go to 58.

54

"Hold it right there, Gash. I'll shoot if I have to." As you say the words, you wonder if they're true. The G'rax freezes, then drops his blaster rifle. He turns toward you and bares his teeth in an animal growl.

That frightens you. You have to ask. "What happened to you?"

"Gnnnaaargh! Hrrarrraaagh vnaaarrgh!"

That doesn't sound like Gash at all. You were right; some Domain plot has controlled his mind. There's no way to talk with him now. You'd better—

Gash lunges for you. For a moment you stand paralyzed by his roar and his bared teeth. But your trigger finger works faster than your brain. The G'rax collapses. Have you ever fired a more painful shot?

"Oh, buddy," you mutter, "that hurt me more than it hurt you."

At that moment the door slides back and the door guard enters. He must have been drawn by the noise.

Startled at what he sees, he raises his blaster rifle—
just in time to be knocked cold by your own shot.
"But that guy," you murmur, "that guy hurts more
than either one of us."

Despite the shower of blaster bolts, no one outside
was alerted by your battle. Anyone who heard it
must have taken the noise for more torture.

The Cetapod moans and rumbles inside its torture
tank. Its incomprehensible speech reverberates in
your stomach.

Of course a torture chamber has hyperlon cord.
You tie up the guards with the strong rope. Then you
release the Cetapod. You may not know who it is, but
if the Domain wanted it imprisoned, there must be a
good reason to let it go! Throwing a series of razor
switches, you watch as the tank bottom splits and
falls away. The Cetapod sinks into the open sea
beneath the city and swims ponderously away.

Now what? Gash has been brainwashed. You'll
have to take Gash away, to be cured by medics of the
Resistance if possible. You need help. You shout,
"Wrench!"

Go to 63.

55

Even on a contraption like the *Rustbucket*, you can
easily evade the Domain's orbital security around Pellaj. Jorth's floating stronghold, the *Ocean Lord*, relies on
its own strong armaments. Because there's nothing else
to defend on Pellaj, the orbital sentries are sparse. You
dive into the nightside atmosphere, out of their sensor
range, and circle around to daylight. You see nothing
but blue-green water everywhere.

Homing in on traffic beacons, you see the stronghold

on the horizon. This city on the water has a long flat landing area as big as a spaceport. Clusters of floating hoops and domes bulge at one end.

In the endless expanse of water you see one other feature: a tiny, barren atoll in the distance, apparently a coral reef. At any rate, it's the only solid surface around.

The Resistance is active on Pellaj, infiltrating the *Ocean Lord* and recruiting Cetapods to the cause. But you can't risk radio contact with the Resistance because the *Rustbucket*'s antiquated radio isn't shielded. Its navicomputer tells you the location of the nearest underwater base. But it's a very old listing, the location has probably changed by now, and how waterproof *is* this crate, anyway?

You'll have to land eventually if you want to find Zygash, and you want to put this poor old ship down on solid land before it shakes to pieces.

If you land on the stronghold, then try to bluff or sneak your way in, go to 60.

If you land on the nearby atoll, go to 31.

If you go underwater, to the last known location of the Resistance base, go to 86.

56

Worldways is the only commercial passenger carrier that serves the Dalorvan Minor system. They run a daily luxury spaceliner to Pellaj, the waterworld. Though it shames you, tourist travel looks like your best bet.

The Worldways counter stands in a neglected corner of the Silverlight spaceport. Once the company was much larger, until an advertising disaster struck. The company executives, based in a province of the

world Fundil, spoke only their own language, Vloor-
ish. They devised a company slogan that meant
something like "You Deserve the Best, and You Get It
On Worldways." This slogan, translated from Vloor-
ish into the galactic common tongue, turned into "It's
Best You Get What You Deserve on Worldways." The
company became a laughingstock, business collapsed, and now Worldways survives by servicing
the backwater routes no other carrier bothers with.

Pricing tickets to Pellaj, you find you haven't got
nearly enough debit markers, and you have no way
to get more. But you have always liked traditional
methods of self-reliance—that is, con games.

The con you come up with is one of the first you
ever ran, when you were a kid trying to get off Carelax to see amazing new worlds. It's still solid after all
this time.

You wait for a likely couple, listening to passersby
chat in a dozen languages. Ah, here come two furry
little Gnomian tourists wearing mate-collars and
laden with luggage. Their beady black eyes stare
around in confusion; Gnomians are often near-
sighted. From what you saw of the Worldways itiner-
ary, they'll pass through Dalorvan Minor on a layover
before heading home to Hibbakuk. "May I help with
that?" you ask charmingly as they waddle into the
commercial terminal.

"*Zhoog? Ah. Og, snut wuggo.*" The female hands a
couple of paper-wrapped parcels up to you. As you
hoped, they assume you're spaceport help.

On the long walk to the Worldways counter, you
chat pleasantly. Hope you enjoyed your stay—isn't
the sky lovely here?—good that folks are still coming
here, even with that scare with the tickets—did you
manage to visit—

"*Zhoog nit winnit?*"

"Oh, yes, you must have been warned before you

arrived. Remember? The experimental nerve-agents impregnated in some spaceliner tickets by accident?"

"*Zhoog? Zhot?*" The male plucks at his hair-fringes nervously.

So you tell them all about it. The Domain wanted to catch traitors in the spaceport ticketing department, but the tickets got passed to the public by mistake. Six thousand dead so far. But don't worry, Gnomians probably haven't been affected on this trip. Unless—well, they haven't had any of the symptoms, you hope? Bad reaction to the local food, homesickness, pheromone secretions that cause the hotel help to act rudely?

"*Zweet, zweet, minot goohi looboogit!*" Both Gnomians pull out their return tickets and fling them away.

Oh, you're sorry! But there's still hope. You'll be able to check the tickets' serial numbers to find whether they're in the contaminated lot. You pick up the tickets, and that's when you try to slip one up your sleeve.

You thought you'd remember that old ticket-switch move to the end of your life, but it's been quite a while. The ticket catches halfway between its envelope and your sleeve, and the Gnomians see it. "*Ho, gonnoto, Tigo, Tigo!*" they cry. From all around the terminal the "*Tigo*"—security guards—come running.

"And after I warned you about nerve-agents, too, you ungrateful little—" No time for bitterness. The guards descend, take your blaster, and ask what's going on. Over the babbling Gnomian tourists you try to explain about your longtime nervous ailment, which makes things in your hands pop up your sleeves. It sounds limp even to you.

Using his weapon, the security supervisor gestures you into an office behind the Worldways ticket counter. The Gnomians he sends on to their boarding gate.

In the office you size up the supervisor. If you had to—just for example—throw him against the wall, slug him, knock him cold, and take his uniform, could you do it? It doesn't look promising.

He says, "Don't bother trying anything. You're Hayl, aren't you?"

Caught! You bid Zygash a silent good-bye.

"After what I'd heard about your rep, I figured you'd be smoother. Well, glad to meet you, anyway, and long live the Resistance. I take it you want a ticket to Pellaj?"

Once you find your vocal cords and thank him, the supervisor leads you to the ticket counter.

He puts you in a line leading to an elderly clerk who looks like he's enjoyed a lot of parties in his life. The man looks vaguely familiar, even under the layers of lubricant from the ship engine. Then you place him, a friend of a friend of Scrobbin, your buddy and sometime partner from the days of smuggling batnip to the shrieker-bats on Froyl.

When you reach the head of the line, you tell him, "I'm trying to get to Pellaj." You make the Resistance code-sign: an inconspicuous brush across the lips with the right middle knuckle.

"Certainly, sir," he says, giving you a knowing look. "Any luggage?" He lets you check your blaster, in the guise of a frigicask of treesblood. "There's room for your robot in the cabin."

The man issues you a first-class ticket to Pellaj with a luxury cabin on the viewport deck. "We ask that you read the ticket instructions before boarding, sir," he tells you. You nod and head for the boarding gate. Along the way you peek at the ticket stub: "DOMAIN PASSWORD: FUSION FURNACE." You make a mental note of that password: "fusion furnace."

You rush for the boarding gate. Entering the hatch just minutes before takeoff, you strap down in your cabin. First class—not bad. Inertial dampers reduce the pressure of lift to no more than a comfy massage. You're happy to see the Resistance is popular on Silverlight!

Worldways may have fallen on hard times, but you can't tell from their colossus-class luxury space cruiser. This great vessel has staterooms, observation decks, a gymnasium and casino, and all the trimmings. And the clientele looks just as high-class. You've seldom ridden this posh.

The drawback is that such a ship is desperately slow. With a long hyperspatial journey ahead, you must decide how to spend your time.

If you try the casino lounge, go to 12.
If you stay in your cabin, go to 16.

57

"Jaspon," you purr into the radio. "Think what you could do with a thousand gross of shirts. What about another statue, maybe a scale version of this ship? I can get those shirts for you."

His angry cry tells you of your mistake. "I hate shirts, do you hear?" Dentoze cries. "*Hate* them! Never again will I cut another sleeve or sew a pocket! My statue is the ultimate disposal of the cursed fabric of my past! You've aggravated me greatly by dredging up these unpleasant memories. For that, I leave you to contemplate your folly."

"No, no, Jaspon, I was only joshing! Listen. I'm big, *very* big, with the Resistance. I know Drewan, the leader, personally."

"So?"

"So, uh—" You decide that Jaspon must want success as an artist. "—So I'm in the pilot's seat for franchises, advertising, promotional arrangements, and publicity. Think of it, Jaspon, your statue could be the Galaxy's biggest tourist attraction! Everyone from a hundred worlds will come out here to see your shirts. I can make it happen for you, Jaspon!"

Silence, for what seems a very long time. Finally, when you're sure you'll drown in your own sweat, he says, "You intrigue me, Hayl. Tell me more."

You start your pitch. "Yessir, once the Resistance wins, I'll set you up with major art dealers—"

"What do you mean, once the Resistance wins?" asks Jaspon.

"Well, you know the Resistance is still fighting the Domain. Of course we'll have to get the Imperials out of power before I can—"

"I knew it! Toying with my ambitions! You shall live to regret this casual manipulation, sir, assuming you regret it quickly. Good-b—"

"No, no, no, no!" Desperate to correct your mistake, you try to laugh blithely. The laugh comes out a dry croak, but you have his attention again. You think of another approach to his vanity. "Heh heh. Heh. You've seen through me, Jaspon. But I know, as you're a man of worldly knowledge, you'll forgive my little tricks. You've forced me to come right down to brass power cores: How much do you want?"

"What?" comes his voice over the radio. "Money? You mean," he says slowly, "you want to buy my statue?"

"I love it! You might say I can't live without it."

"Well, well, I'm honestly surprised, Hayl. I mean, I didn't think the public would appreciate me so soon. You know, this is exciting, but I deserve a fair price. I want 120 million debit markers."

You currently have maybe 120 DMs, never mind the million. But he doesn't know that. You have to convince him you're rich enough to make *him* rich. "I'll give you 90 million, Jaspon, and you pay the transport costs to a major orbital museum, *plus* all associated publicity costs to guarantee an audience of at least one hundred million people."

"You drive a hard bargain, sir," he says loftily, while you hang outside the airlock in blackness. As though you could drive any kind of bargain! "But 90 million is a pittance. How about 110?" Sweating, you finish the act: You talk him down to 105 million and publicity costs. "Deal, sir!" Jaspon says joyfully. "Come inside and we'll celebrate with a toast."

In eDrive Jaspon sits quietly for a while, then turns to you with sad eyes. "No, Hayl, I can't part with it. The statue means more to me than a family member." Of course his change of heart leaves you devastated (at least that's what you tell him), but you agree to remain friends.

You arrive safely at the Dvaad mining operation, a large asteroid pocked with craters and shafts. Jaspon gives the security codes that admit the *Small Waist* to the Domain landing base. He introduces you as "his assistant in charge of mining equipment," and Wrench the maintenance bot hardly needs a cover story. The Imperials let you both pass without much more than a second glance.

Once past the initial checkpoints, Jaspon claps you on the shoulder. "Well met, Hayl. I hope your Resistance can find another artist to serve as its voice and inspiration."

"Jaspon, just knowing you has given me all kinds of inspiration," you say. To yourself you think, I'm inspired to avoid miners for the rest of my life. You and Wrench take leave of Jaspon politely but quickly.

You're free to look around the Dvaad asteroid base.

Go to 84.

58

At first sight, nothing distinguishes Dvaad from any other small-change mine in the galaxy. Approaching from space, you see rounded refinery towers, waste sluices open to the vacuum of space, and the usual railgun ramp that accelerates buckets of metal to orbital factories. Dirty gray domes, houses for mine personnel, cluster beneath one tower. The whole mine looks so grimy it might have grown from the living rock of the asteroid.

Nothing unusual. But the Domain runs Dvaad, and that makes it unusual. Ordinarily the Domain would never bother with a little operation like this.

Piloting your ship skillfully among the other asteroids in this belt, you consider your approach. If they learn who you are, the Domains will arrest you instantly. Of course, that would be the most direct way to enter the colony. You can imagine the conversation:

"Uh, Traffic Control, incoming ship requesting landing clearance, over."

"Incoming ship, identify yourself."

"Notorious smuggler Rogan Hayl of the Resistance."

A very long pause. "Uh, say again?"

Yeah, right. Not even you feel quite that gutsy. A stealthy approach it is.

If you're flying the Resistance courier ship *Rustbucket*, go to 30.

If you are piloting Jaspon Dentoze's mining ship, the *Small Waist*, go to 33.

59

"When the G'rax fell to the Subverter's influence," says Jorth, "I knew you would eventually follow him

here. Now the Subverter is gone, evidently. Yet I retain the G'rax just the same."

The governor pushes a button on the arm of his bodychair. A wall panel slides back, revealing a large metal disk that rotates slowly on the wall. The disk is engraved with pain nodes that flicker with electric pulses. On the disk lies Zygash, spread-eagle, strapped to its edges by his wrists and ankles.

Jorth presses another button. On the disk, the pulses increase, and Gash howls in pain. You rush at Jorth, but the soldiers knock you back to the floor.

Chuckling quietly, Jorth continues. "Yes, Hayl, this is a fine time for the Domain. The leader of your Resistance on this world, the Cetapod called Haurrassith, will eventually be persuaded to cooperate with us in destroying your Resistance."

"You wish! The Cetapods will never help the Domain while you hunt them like beasts."

Jorth says lightly. "These creatures are too valuable to be treated as intelligent beings. If this Haurrassith, as its name is, tries to stir up Resistance sympathies among its fellow swimmers, then of course the Domain must capture and imprison it.

"I must say," he continues, brushing his serpent-skin tunic and sighing, "that it is quite gratifying to hold at my mercy a creature a thousand times larger and stronger than myself. This Haurrassith is now in the torture tanks, and expected to break very shortly, I believe. And you and your friend are soon to go to one who requested you."

"Yeah? Who's that?"

Jorth smiles and starts to reply. But all at once, the entire room shakes violently! Art objects topple from tables, hanging tapestries flap outward, and soldiers fall around you. Across a tilting floor you roll to the bodychair.

The shaking stops, or—the thought fills you with

dread—has it only paused? Before either Jorth, the guards, or you yourself understand what happened, you've stolen Jorth's own blaster and are holding him hostage. You scream your demands: "Drop your rifles and free Gash, or Baron Slimeball here gets a new skylight to air out his brain!"

Jorth gasps. "Do—Do as—Follow his or-orders!" he stammers.

The guards rush to unstrap Zygash from the electrode disk. Wrench, the robot, wheels over to join you both. Meanwhile, you and everyone wonder the same thing: What caused the shaking? And could it happen again?

Go to 85 to find out.

60

Landing your Resistance ship in the very stronghold of the Domain governor? Well, it's certainly a gutsy, Rogan Hayl kind of move.

But it goes smoothly. You check through the Resistance ship's library of false clearance codes, pick a likely entry, and radio it in with one of your standard cover stories. The controller handles it routinely, you get clearance to land, and in you go.

Once in the landing area, you smoothly exit the ship and walk right into a platoon of Domain soldiers, all with blaster rifles carefully aimed at you. They weren't fooled for a moment.

Not even you are crazy enough to fight in this situation. As they march you to Baron Jorth for interrogation, you ask, "What did I do wrong?"

A trooper tilts his visored head in what you take to be amusement. "Nothing. If your scaly buddy hadn't tipped us off—"

"That's enough, soldier!" barks the commander.

That's enough—to send your mind spinning. Gash turned you in! Can it be true? You keep marching, hands on your head, heart in your mouth.

Go to 88.

61

Chasma Hoyd is growing hysterical. You grab her by the billowing folds of her gown and pull her toward you. Your hand meets her cheek with a meaty *thup!* With your face about a finger-length from hers, you say calmly, "Calm down. Everyone is looking at you. You're only embarrassing yourself."

It works. She settles down and pulls haughtily away. But you can tell she doesn't like you one bit! She scoops up her winnings and waddles off.

The Ilirishi keep poking around in the spaceliner for a while. Finally their curiosity (if that's what it was) is satisfied, and they depart as suddenly as they arrived, shrinking away into the nothingness of eSpace. The rest of the trip is uneventful, and eventually you arrive at Pellaj.

Go to 10.

62

Hitting the torture tank's release switches, you watch the tank bottom open to the water beneath. The Cetapod sinks down and swims away. You can make out the forms of other Cetapods below. "Boon companions," you mutter to Gash. "I'd hate to think what they have planned for this place."

But in moments you're forced to think about it. The entire stronghold shakes with the force of the Cetapod underwater assault. Gash grabs a blaster and growls, *"Vhhhaaaraaungghh!"*

"All right, lead the way," you reply. You exit the chamber only to find the corridor swarming with frightened bureaucrats, technicians, and guards. The shaking continues, and no one pays attention as you follow Gash to the shipyard and landing area.

Wrench the robot joins you in the hallway. "Water depth on Pellaj averages eight kilometers, Captain Hayl. Do you have a plan to avoid a dismal, watery grave?"

"Shut up and follow me." You only wish you did have a plan.

At every step of the journey to the shipyard you hear screams, explosions, and the crash of collapsing ceilings. Smoke fills the corridors. Cetapods thrust upward through the floor and leap out of the sea through walls and windows. Every collision leaves a hole big enough for a loaderbot.

Then you hear, or rather feel, a muffled explosion below, and the ground drops from under you. Everyone in the hallways falls shrieking to the floor. You're the first back on your feet because you know what that explosion meant: A Cetapod sacrificed itself destroying the antigrav generators.

"This place is going under, Gash! Step on it! You too, Wrench!"

"Right with you, sir."

The G'rax looks around in confusion. *"Hnnnaaauu-urrrgh hwaaar!"*

"Oh, great!" You can't blame him for getting lost because you can't see the direction signs through the smoke either. You just blunder along, keeping hold of one of Gash's left arms. The smoke gets so thick sometimes that you can't even tell which left arm.

For a tense time you fear you won't get out before the city sinks. Then you emerge on a concrete canopy that extends into the sea, a "wharf" for water landings.

Sea-skimmers are all around, as well as larger seacraft that you couldn't pilot alone. The entire canopy is rippling like a canvas tarpaulin, and tremendous waves are washing up almost to your feet. You'd better grab a skimmer before there's nowhere left to stand.

Go to 74.

63

Sad to look down at Gash's unconscious body, but you don't dare wake him up. Still, you need some way of transporting him out of this place, and Wrench can do it.

"Wrench, carry him."

"Yes, sir." Wrench easily hoists Zygash's bulk, but you still worry for your unconscious friend. You head for the door, with robot and G'rax in tow. Now, how to get past the surveillance cameras and blow this joint—?

Krrrrboooommmm! A muffled explosion sounds somewhere below, and the floor drops from beneath your feet. The entire *Ocean Lord* has sunk a meter or more into the water! Now the walls tremble, and you hear a chain of louder explosions, elsewhere in the citadel. You think of the freed Cetapod. "C'mon, sounds like we have to get out of here fast," you tell the robot.

You enter the hallway. The detention area is in total confusion, with troopers and robots and personnel rushing from place to place seemingly without reason. In the frenzy, no one notices you and Wrench making your way to a ship hangar.

Looking down side hallways, you see many fires. Ahead and behind are milling crowds. Everywhere you hear shouts, alarms, and destruction. Smells of smoke and spilled fuel make you move even faster. The *Ocean Lord*, Baron Jorth's mighty stronghold, is sinking!

In the chaos, you lose your sense of direction. You hope you're still bearing for the ships, but smoke obscures directional signs. You see a sign over a crowded hallway: To SHIPYARD. Any port in a storm, you think. As it were.

Go to 65.

64

Chasma Hoyd's squawking panic is almost as interesting as the Ilirishi. Arms flailing, gown flying, hairstyle disintegrating, she turns this way and that, looking for an exit and finding nothing but another white blob growing in her path. Her antics distract you, and something moist flops down over your head and upper body. You're absorbed by an Ilirishi!

Go to 66.

65

While decks list beneath your feet, while staircases collapse and antigrav elevators spiral off through the atrium and crash into support pillars, while explosions come ever more often, ever closer—you emerge onto the open expanse of the shipyard.

Many spaceships stand here, tilting back and forth

gently as though the *Ocean Lord* sailed rough waters. Yet the bright sun and the calm sea tells you that this is no storm.

"Come on!" you shout to Wrench. "We've got to get a ship before this place sinks!" Making your way across the shaking deck, you see a couple of likely spacecraft.

As you start to choose a ship, a blow from behind sends you smashing into the deck. Zygash has awakened, snapped the hyperlon cord binding him, and attacked you!

The stronghold is moments away from a grave two kilometers deep. Even so, you can't bring yourself to fight your best friend, even to save him—or yourself. This is Gash, who saved your life when you both took the Initiation Walk back on Carelax, almost twenty standard years ago. Gash, who helped you put down the first payment on the *Prosperogenesis*, who got it out of hock for you and stole it back from the con man you lost it to in a game of suns-or-moons.

You know the G'rax can beat you into the ground. But for the life of you—a literal phrase in this case— you can't raise a hand against him. "Please, Gash, don't do this—"

A sweeping double punch from the G'rax's scaly left fists sends you plummeting sidelong to the deck. Water laps around your bleeding head. How long before the stronghold sinks? It doesn't matter, you realize. Zygash stands over you, ready to strike the Last Fourfold Punch hallowed in G'rax chants and legends.

"Do it," you tell him through bloody lips. "Then get out fast, before this place drags you under. Do it, Gash." You close your eyes.

For a long moment you hear nothing. Then Gash grumbles uncertainly. Again. And then he sweeps you up and hugs you, tight enough to cause shooting pain in your already-bruised ribs. "Oww! Hey, you're back! Gash, this is terrific! Oww!"

"*Gnnnaaraarrgh vaaraaagh! Hnnnarrgh vnugh vnaarr!*" says Gash, overcome with remorse.

"Okay, okay, I forgive you, I understand. Unless you break my back.—Come on now, time for a tearful reunion later. Let's get out before we drown."

Go to 4.

66

Inside the Ilirishi, you suddenly begin thinking thoughts you can't understand, thoughts you can't even put into language. You reel with ideas of whole-ness, the unity of past and future, and the whole galaxy stretched out before you like a sheet.

These must be the thought processes of the creature as it examines you. You hear a trickle of energy across your skin and all through you. Somehow you hear music being created by every passenger aboard the ship—in every creature on the worlds beneath you—everywhere in the galaxy. This, you realize, must be the Music of the Spheres!

You hear the Music as an infinite symphony, with each melody a world. Beneath the melodic lines rolls a powerful, dissonant bass line: the Discord Strains. Here and there you detect sources of that discord. One loud source, far away, you somehow identify as Emperor Darenon Morione. Somewhat nearer, you hear a quavering discordant note that conjures in your mind the face of clan ruler Duke Carabajal. A third, nearby, emanates from an asteroid mine in the Dalorvan Minor system: Dvaad. You shrink away from its inhuman presence.

The end of this visit takes you by surprise. Without warning, the Ilirishi plops you down in your cabin and leaves. You lie there grappling with what happened until the spaceliner arrives at Pellaj.

Go to 10.

67

You've removed the danger of the Subverter, but where is Zygash? If he joined the Domain, and then the hive-mind's control broke, Gash is probably amid enemies now.

A factscreen lying on the *Genesis* console, left over from the Domain's examination of your ship, indicates that the "informant" who provided the ship— Gash—went to the waterworld of Pellaj, in this same system.

"What do you know about Pellaj?" you ask Wrench, the robot.

"Not much, sir. On Silverlight I met several robots that had worked briefly at the Domain's Pellaj base, the *Ocean Lord*. They said that on Pellaj they were prone to rust."

"That sure does help, Wrench."

"You're welcome, Captain Hayl."

The eSpace journey is brief, just long enough for you to work up a nasty temper. When you think of how this Subverter molded your best friend's mind and made the Resistance think him a traitor, you dig your fingers into the arms of your pilot's chair and growl. Well, now you've got your own ship back, the fastest in the galaxy, and you're ready to take on anybody or anything.

The Domain is in trouble now.

Go to 10.

68

Gash stares as you power up the translation device, but you ignore his confusion. More a subsonic vibration than a sound, the Cetapod's voice is so deep you can hardly hear it, but so loud it's deafening. The Resistance translation device turns the creature's words into cultured human speech and plays it in your ear.

"This one, smallest of swimmers in the vast world, is eager Haurrassith," says the Cetapod. "Free this one, little thing, to swim suspended with the fellows in the world. The fellows plan life-struggle-sacrifice upon this place above the world. This one must join them."

Gash growls quizzically. "Sounds like the other

Cetapods are planning a raid to free him," you explain. You speak into the device, and your words become howls. "When will this happen?"

The Cetapod's eye shows understanding. "This one feels the fellows approaching. In the stroke of a youngling's tail, the fellows will—"

Wham! The stronghold's floor shakes beneath your feet. "That's the start of it," you tell Gash as you run for the tank controls.

Go to 62.

69

What password? You tell the soldier the first thing that enters your mind. "Incorrect," says the guard.

"Incorrect? Something's wrong with the password update system, I'll go look into it." You turn to go, but every instinct says the guard is wise to you. The instincts prove right as his rifle fires behind you, just an instant before he says "Halt!"

The noise from your first exchange of shots alerts the rest of the stronghold. Riot gas fills the corridor. You're caught and taken to Baron Jorth.

Go to 88.

70

The Worldways cruiser drops gracefully through the atmosphere, heading toward the floating Domain stronghold, the *Ocean Lord*.

The *Ocean Lord* has a long, flat landing area bigger than some entire spaceports, with a pile of white domes and spires rising at one end. The building nearest your landing point is the customs office.

The captain announces customs procedures, including inspection and identification. Hmm . . . this could be tricky. But you've been on the shady side of the law long enough that you've checked out alternate exits from the spacecraft. When the ship lands, you can risk going through customs, or try sneaking out through the supply ports, bypassing customs.

If you go through customs, go to 82.
If you sneak past customs, go to 35.

71

Strapped into your upholstered pilot's seat, you practically drool over the state-of-the-art controls on the yacht's front panel. What a dream machine! The liftoff was smooth, the rate of climb dizzying.

Through the left viewport you look down on the seas of Pellaj. Far below, the *Ocean Lord* is breaking into pieces, and the pieces are sinking. From this altitude the Domain seems only a disappearing mote in the great sea of Resistance spirit. Nice thought!

Zygash is back in the main cabin. You're looking forward to a peaceful reunion.

You know, it seems awfully quiet back in the main cabin. You look aft—and there's Baron Jorth, short and fat and pale and ruthless, pointing a blaster at Gash! His pouchy eyes are bulging, and his breath is ragged. His limbs, with their strange bulges at elbows and shoulders, are trembling with emotion.

"You are not to consider any wild actions, you G'rax," Jorth hisses. "I am in control here." He probably intends to shoot you and Gash, then pilot the ship to another Domain base.

You pull back out of sight, your mind racing. You

can't risk firing your blaster aboard ship. You might blow out a hole in the cabin, and your air with it. But Jorth looks crazy enough that he wouldn't hesitate to fire his own weapon. What to do?

You might send the ship through a risky rolling maneuver to throw Jorth off-balance. Nothing else looks practical except some kind of direct attack.

To try maneuvering the ship, go to 9.
If you ask Wrench the robot to help you, go to 23.
If you leap at Jorth with fists flying, go to 28.

72

You've learned, many times over, the value of a well-placed bribe. But it's hard to think what such an alien being could be interested in.

This thing seems to have primitive needs. "What do you eat here, anything besides this green glop? How about some *real* food?"

The hive-mind considers. *Is the humanbeing offering itself?*

"Uh, no."

We partake only of the milk of the cattle. We have all the cattle we can use. The cattle partake of the growths we bring from deep within the world. The humanbeings know not to disturb these growths, or we will destroy all. We eat, we maintain, we survive until the worlds meet and we breed. It is the way and the rhythm of ten million orbits.

You think to yourself, What a fun life. "You know, speaking of breeding, this asteroid isn't so big. I'll bet after a while you're going to breed enough new little bugs to fill this place up to the craters. Join the Resistance, and we'll give you more asteroids—even a planet. There're plenty of them."

The Subverter isn't impressed. *We do not breed as the*

humanbeings do. We are sufficient in this world. When our world encounters another, in the expanse of time, we will join with the colony there, merge, and in merging, die. The worlds will divide into many, and the young will spread.

You don't understand much of this offbeat breeding cycle, but anyway, the Kakklakks are not interested in more living space.

Try again! "Well, how about this. If you help the Resistance, we can win victory over the Domain. You'll be renowned throughout the galaxy. Every intelligent race will owe you a tremendous debt of thanks. What I could do with that kind of—well, never mind. You could be that famous!"

To what purpose? asks the voice in your mind.

"Uh, well, gratitude, friends, lots of money if you play it right, the affections of fellow members of your species, uh—" As you speak, you gradually realize that none of these concepts mean anything to a hive-mind that isn't even sentient most of the time. You trail off.

Hmmm. You look at the pile of natives, all pulsing in unison. "Are you, maybe, um, lonely?" you ask, with a casual air.

We are unified in one intellect.

"Would you be interested in finding some other intellect to pile up with? Maybe some other Kakklakks?"

A tremendous clacking. *The humanbeing offers a union with another colony?* The pile begins to throb. *Is this so? Is this within the humanbeing's—within your power?*

Bingo! "Well, I don't promise anything. But the Resistance can pull off some amazing feats. We might be able to scare up another asteroid full of bugs, if you ask nicely."

Tell us how! Tell us!

How would the Resistance do this? You're not

really sure. Yet you decide to bull your way through. "Hey, I can take some of you Kakklakks on my ship, the *Prosperogenesis*, and ferry them around this asteroid system. Nothing to it, I do it all the time." (Of course, you haven't found the *Genesis* yet, but the hive-mind doesn't know that.)

The Kakklakks receive your offer of transport enthusiastically, to put it mildly. Duke Carabajal never taught them the concept of taking a vehicle off-planet, surely because he didn't want the hive-mind to get any ideas.

"Happy to be of service," you tell the Subverter. "But I don't know where the ship is right now. The Domain brought it to this mining colony not long ago, but—"

Ship is in ship area. One of us has seen it arrive. Humanbeing will follow. The natives fall out of their pile, rearrange their shells, and march in single file up an exit tunnel. Following, you eventually reach the human area of the complex. The residents seem to be accustomed to the sight of a line of Kakklakks marching through their tunnels.

This series of tunnels has an antiseptic air, and judging from the robots and technicians walking around, it's some kind of laboratory area. The Domain must have set it up to study the Subverter, but it's too large for just that. What else could they be studying?

The Kakklakks lead you to a large underground hangar, and you find out what else they study: your ship! The *Prosperogenesis* has been systematically dismantled, its circuitry and systems arranged by size and type across the floor of the hangar. The Domain must have wanted to know how you souped it up. "Oh, my ship, my ship, what am I gonna do?" you moan to yourself.

There in the hangar, beneath the shell of your beloved beauty, a hundred or so Kakklakks reform

into the Subverter hive-mind. *Ship is here, correct?
Humanbeing takes us away now.*

"Incorrect," you sigh. "Ship is busted. Completely
taken to pieces. Don't work no more."

Ship cannot carry us to another Kakklakk colony?

"Ship cannot carry a one-note tune until it's put
together again." You don't even see a maintenance
robot around, except Wrench, and this is much too
big a job for him alone. And, of course, you're deep
inside an enemy base, where they're likely to frown
on things like putting together Resistance ships. How
can you reassemble the *Genesis*?

Then the Subverter says, *We will make ship workable.
Stand still.* That's when matters grow much weirder
than you could have imagined.

Go to 36.

73

You supervise the robots as they continue the
repair of the *Genesis*. You hide from the guards and
techs that occasionally wander by. According to the
ship manifest you found on a factscreen in the cockpit, the operation was supposed to continue with
only robot supervision until the entire ship was dismantled. No human is checking on the progress, so
no human can catch you reversing it. Serves them
right for trusting robots, you think.

With the last circuit modules plugged in and the
last retaining bolts tightened, the *Genesis* looks ready
to fly once more. Your heart is full as you finally walk
the floors of your own, your *only* ship.

"Work has been completed, sir," says a robot.

"Terrific job. Take the day off. You've earned it."

Of course you're eager to leave—but you're in an

underground hangar, with no obvious way to get out. There's no ceiling port; the techs must have partly dismantled the ship just to get it in here. You're not going to take it apart again to get it out. And naturally you can't jump to eDrive down here.

There is one answer that most people wouldn't think of, but you, Rogan Hayl, leap to it almost at once. You'll shoot your way out!

Go to 83.

74

Grabbing a two-seat skimmer, you and Gash launch out over the waves. Gash easily carries Wrench the robot. Behind you, the Domain's stronghold begins to break apart.

From a distance, it looks like nothing much has gone wrong on the *Ocean Lord*. Smoke billows from a few ports, and you hear alarms even out here. Otherwise it could be a peaceful city on the water.

Then you see how far it lists to one side. And the fractures running through most of the domes. And the foundering watercraft, pulled under by their own bowlines. Rumbling noises build and chase you across the water. The domes and hoops pull apart from one another like clouds, and for a moment they seem to float on their own in the surf.

A sudden explosion rips through the city. All the structures, so small at this range, topple into the water and sink in moments. The long spaceport landing field tilts up, up, then slides straight down like a knife, and Baron Jorth's mighty *Ocean Lord* sinks from view forever.

But one survivor launched from that sinking deck, moments before the disaster. A shining space-yacht, a

powerful streamlined ship, has lifted off and now swerves smoothly to approach you. Gash identifies it with a growl, but you already knew. "Jorth," you whisper.

No one else could own such a handsome ship. No one but a Domain governor could have the pure ruthless survival instinct needed to escape under such conditions. Jorth screams over the ship's public hailer: "You! You've taken my city! Now I shall take you as well!" Even though the yacht is still far out of range, it begins a strafing fire of blaster bolts. And there you are, right in its path, on the open sea.

"Another tight spot," you say. You might dive underwater, but the sinking stronghold will create treacherous currents. "Hold tight!" you shout to the others, twisting the skimmer's throttle to maximum. Sheets of water fly up as you skip across the sea. On either side, waves sizzle and spatter under Jorth's strafing fire.

"*Hnnnarrrannggh!*" Gash shouts, reaching past you to grab the handlebars. Your struggles with him pull the skimmer to one side, and that's all that saves you as the yacht zooms by, hardly a body-length overhead. Thruster backwash slices deep into the water; if you'd stayed on the previous path, Jorth would have fried you.

As it is, a wave of foamy seawater flips the skimmer half over. Deafened by the yacht's passage, you can't hear Gash's growls or the whine of the gyroscopes as they pull the skimmer upright. The vehicle sits unmoving on the surface. "Is it over?" you say, disoriented. "Are we dead now?"

Not quite yet, for Jorth is turning around for another strafing run, this time head-on. "Crazy!" you shout in frustration. "He could be escaping into orbit! He could go to another Domain base! But no, he has to stick around to kill us, through *pure spite!*" Angry at the injustice, you twist the handlebars, bringing the battered skimmer back up to speed.

With switchbacks and rapid zigzags, you dodge Jorth's withering cannon fire. But how long can you keep this up? There's nothing but open water ahead of you, and with every maneuver, the yacht closes the distance between you. Your only choice is to dive underwater and risk the currents. "Hold tight!" you tell the others.

"*Rnnnagh rnnnagh!*"

"So what if I said it already? You pick now to complain that I repeat myself?" With the twist of a handgrip you send the skimmer diving undersea. Instantly a hundred cross-currents batter the vehicle. The whole sea is in turmoil.

From a distance, you hear the screams of Cetapods, off where a white-hot glow—the power generator of the destroyed *Ocean Lord*—sinks slowly into the deep. Those screams: Are they warnings? Gash must think so. He's pounding at the skimmer's dome, growling that you should get out of the area immediately, wishing he were back home on Carelax with his wives.

You shoot away from the turbulence and soon reach clear waters. "Looks like we got away—" you begin, and then Jorth's space-yacht plunges underwater just behind you. "*Hrrnt!*" cries Gash.

"I *am* gunning it!" But it's hopeless to try outrunning a starcruiser in your little skimmer. The yacht closes, not firing. You wonder why he hasn't blown you away, until you realize the brutal truth: Jorth intends to run you down!

You're moving at top speed, but it only delays the inevitable. Nowhere nearby to hide, nowhere to run to—you glance back, long enough to see Jorth's ugly face in the yacht's front viewport. He's cackling.

What a lousy sight to exit on, you think. At that moment, long reddish tentacles lash out from below, on either side of the yacht. Looking down, you see bulky shadows that can only be Cetapods!

Dwarfing the yacht, the gigantic creatures tear away weapon pods and thruster ports, pull off airlock doors, and strike through viewports. With ruthless efficiency, they tear the craft to pieces, and everything inside as well. You think, Good-bye, Jorth! What a great sight to exit on.

Resistance skimmers pull up on either side of you. After that, it seems only moments until you're at the Resistance base and drinking hot singflower tea. Gash is thirsty for a mug of treesblood, but—"Sorry, I'd guess the nearest cask is light-years away," says Tandon Rey, the Pellaj Resistance commander. "Still, if anybody deserves a reward, it's you two."

"And their robot," Wrench adds.

"With Jorth out of the way," Tandon continues, "the Cetapods can live in peace again. The Resistance can establish defenses to keep the Domain from moving back in here. Good work."

"I just wanted to save my friend," you tell him.

"We should all have friends like you, Hayl."

After a lot of thank-yous on both sides, you're ready to leave Pellaj.

If you have already been to the Dvaad asteroid mine in this adventure, go to 93.

If you have not yet gone to Dvaad, go to 25.

75

The three technicians enter the lab in a group. They're unarmed, but you have to take them out fast to keep them from sounding the alarm.

The first two fall like sacks of radium slugs. But your third shot goes wild, and the surviving tech runs screaming. He'll have the guards down your throat in a moment. You grab the eDrive unit from the table. As you head out the hatchway, you hear a speaker click on, and then *Brrrnnnnnnggg! Whooop-whoooop! Nee-nah nee-nah nee-nah. . . .*

That's an alarm if you ever heard one. There must be fifty claxons blaring through this tunnel. Struggling with the drive's weight, you stumble down to the *Prosperogenesis*. You hear running feet close behind.

Throwing the drive unit aboard the ship, and hoping searchers will miss it amid the clutter, you pull up a floor panel and dive into one of your concealed smuggling bays. You hear boots marching through the ship, searching everywhere inside and around it. You can't make out voices, but the guards must have decided you ran elsewhere, because they leave.

After a time you emerge from hiding and continue rebuilding your ship.

Go to 73.

76

You give the soldier your password. He nods and steps aside as the door slides back. You saunter through.

The huge chamber beyond is lined with machinery and gantryways. White panels near the high ceiling provide pale light, but tanks of liquid and masses of crates and barrels make the room a gloomy place. You hear the hum of machines, the rumbling moan of a Cetapod trapped in the largest tank, and the growl of a G'rax.

In front of the Cetapod's tank you see one Domain soldier—and Zygash beside him, carrying a Domain blaster rifle. Gash looks just as he always did, a scaly purple giant with four huge arms and a wide mouth full of sharp teeth.

Whatever your mind knows, your heart says Gash can't really be a Domain flunky. You want to believe he's putting on an act. You get a cover story ready as you approach, thinking Gash will play along. The G'rax sees you, growls a warning to the guard, and both raise their blaster rifles!

You dart behind a line of barrels. Zygash isn't your enemy, but you know the soldier sure is. You take careful aim, pull the trigger, and blam! The guard falls back, knocked out cold with your first shot.

Zygash snarls and fires at you! His first shot hits a barrel, yet it hurts as though it actually hit you. Your best friend is now your enemy.

You can't escape. You must decide whether or not to fire on Gash; he's firing on you!

If you fire at Gash, go to 54.
If you try to reason with him, go to 51.

77

The liftoff from Silverlight in Jaspon Dentoze's mining ship, the *Small Waist*, is none too smooth. You grit your teeth at each bump and every nervous swerve, thinking of how much better you could do. But the miner reaches orbit and jumps to eDrive without incident.

Though Dentoze has appointed it nicely, for a mining craft, his ship is still built on the standard model: one small circular chamber opening directly from the cockpit, with one sleeper berth in back. You sit in a jury-rigged passenger seat facing the central life-support unit, like a camper huddling close to a campfire. Oh, well, at least the gravity's fine.

Jaspon leaves the controls and comes back to talk. He assigns Wrench to an out-of-the-way corner. He gives you a few minor duties of monitoring and maintenance, more from politeness than need. As a traveling companion, your real job is talking and listening.

Mainly you listen. "I am enthused about new career prospects," says Dentoze as he chatters about his life. "Once a much put-upon designer of clothing, now a miner, soon—who knows?—an artist. It is my choice. The choices of life determine what we are, don't you think?" You nod amiably.

You have no trouble getting Dentoze to elaborate on his life story. "I designed shirts and waistcoats for the Aditori, the natives of Aditor in the Wexendian system. They all have at least six arms apiece, you know.

The more arms one has, the higher its caste. Those wealthy ones—nice people, of course, and good customers, but have you ever designed a shirt with twelve arms? No, I thought not. Exhausting work.

"But the infuriating part was the way they would change my design! Here's some high-class Aditori paying me large amounts to create something for him, and I do a perfectly fine job, and then he takes it and *changes my work*! Why do these flat-headed brain-dead plutocrats bother asking me to invest my hard work and creativity, when they'll just *ruin* it after I'm done?" Jaspon has worked himself into a fury. His ranting makes a strange sight.

"It sounds very sad," you murmur consolingly. "*Tch, tch*. Yes, indeed. So, when do we arrive at Dvaad?"

"We're stopping on the way for a scenic view," he says, startling you. Before you can ask what he means, the *Small Waist* suddenly drops out of eDrive.

The drop comes much too soon, taking you off guard. Jaspon slips smoothly into the tiny cockpit and sighs contentedly. You rush up to ask what's happened—and stop.

Outside the *Small Waist*, in deep space, floats a gigantic statue. Thousands of sheets of white fabric hang from a sculpted wire frame. The statue fills your entire view from the forward viewport. It resembles—no, it can't be!

"My self-portrait," says Jaspon. "Isn't it magnificent? An auspicious debut for my new career as interstellar sculptor. It fills my soul to gaze upon it. Ahh."

"Uhh. That fabric—it's—?"

"Shirts, yes. When I retired from garment design I had a large stock remaining. What more appropriate material to indicate the artist's origins?" Abruptly he sits up. "Maker's teeth! Look at my nose!"

He means the statue's nose. A meteoroid must

have struck the statue, because the tip of its nose is
barren of fabric. The hole gapes like a third nostril.

Dentoze's own nostrils flare. "Monstrous! Obscene!
This insult must be repaired immediately. Hayl, give
me your shirt!"

"What?"

"I shall use your shirt to repair the injury. Come,
why do you hesitate?"

"I guess I've never been in quite this situation
before."

Go to 46.

78

What to say? What to use? Your gaze lights on a
gas mask, hanging on a nearby rack. You pull it down
and on, in one smooth motion, just as three technicians enter. "Out, out!" you say, voice muffled
through the mask. "Contamination. Temporarily
closed off. Should have it cleaned up soon. Don't
breathe the stuff."

The techs turn pale and run. "It's your formula,
Borlis," says one. "I knew you shouldn't have over-
pressurized that tank." They squabble as they flee
down the tunnel.

They won't be fooled for long. You rush in and
grab your eDrive system. It looks intact.

One corner of the lab holds some unusual displays:
wall screens and scale models showing the buglike
natives of this asteroid. Looking at printouts, you see
numerous references to the insectoid Kakklakks.

You've got your eDrive system. Time to get out and
take it to the *Genesis*.

Go to 73.

79

You give the soldier your password. He nods and steps aside as the door slides back. You saunter through.

Go to 18.

80

You've wandered into a twisting network of tunnels deep in the asteroid. The passages curve weirdly in all directions and glow dimly with phosphorescence. Some spiral downward, bringing echoes from far away. Is this entire world hollow?

The atmosphere thickens and warms as you walk. The ground grows rocky and uneven, and Wrench the robot finds it tough going. "Sir, I'd like to wait here, if I may," it says. "But don't worry about me. If you happen to fall into deadly danger and die a horrible death, I can find my way to the mining colony and work there."

"How comforting, Wrench. See you later." You don't mind leaving the bot; you travel more quickly alone. You pass through large barren caverns, squeeze through crevasses, and climb rockfalls. The white buglike natives scamper across your path more often.

At last, in a gigantic empty cavern, with an acidic smell strong in your nostrils and no sounds audible but the *chikk*ing and *chukk*ing of the natives, you know you're hopelessly lost.

One of the insects crawls along ahead, over a rockfall at the base of a high cliff. "Hey, little buddy," you ask it, "I don't suppose you know where we are?" Like all the others, the creature seems not to notice you. You say, "If you're intelligent, you do a top-notch job of hiding it."

You decide to follow the insect native. Maybe it's going to the mining complex. You crawl over the rockfall after the native—and with a rumble of sliding rock, the pile of boulders gives way beneath you. You're falling!

You roll down a steep passage, grabbing at other falling objects for stability. Landing with a grunt in a pile of rocks, you check for injuries. You're intact, though heavily bruised.

You reach out for a handhold, and grab something moist and squishy. "Yaah!" you cry, leaping up. You were lying next to a giant legless creature with many-faceted eyes, waving antennae, and a globular body covered with sacs of greenish fluid. It's some kind of horrible bug.

And you're in a cavern full of them. They adhere to the walls and floor everywhere. The white multi-

legged insect natives run among them. A white native taps on a bug's full sac, and on that signal the fluid rushes out. The white insect catches the fluid in its mouth, then staggers away to dump the fluid into a natural rock cistern. This is a bubbling cauldron with an awful stench at the other end of the cavern.

"Chaukk, katchuk!" A native is crawling around your feet. And now another, and still more. All the natives have seen you, and from the way they cluck and snap their mandibles, they seem disturbed. You look for exits, but the slope is unclimbable, and every other tunnel is beyond the swarming natives.

They crawl on one another in excitement—some kind of instinctive response? The pile grows with every moment, to dozens . . . almost a hundred . . . more. The creatures writhe, then quiet down as the stack increases. Their white shells split along the ridges. Each native's many legs thrust down inside the shells of many neighbors.

They begin to clack in unison, and that's when you really want to leave. Suddenly you hear a strange voice in your mind, speaking in your own language: *Humanbeing! What does it here?*

This is too much! You leap over one of the horrible fluid-making bugs and race for the nearest tunnel. And then you stop as a sinister presence appears in your mind. *The humanbeing does not wish to escape*, it says.

You turn back as though pulled by strings. You stand frozen before the pulsing heap of natives.

This deed we recently learned to do to humanbeings, says the voice—the mind of the natives, one intelligence shared among many bodies. The whole pile pulsates rhythmically. *We are the kakklakks, but the humanbeings know us as the Subverter.*

"A hive-mind," you whisper. There aren't many in

the entire galaxy, and a good thing too. When many creatures share the same consciousness, they can overwhelm most opponents. All too often, they treat all living creatures not in the hive as "opponents."

The humanbeing intrudes on our most-private food-place, says the hive-mind. *Why? The other humanbeings do not come here, except the old humanbeing and his servants wise in the Music.* Here the hive-mind duplicates, uncannily, the voice of the clan ruler of this sector. "Duke Carabajal!" you say, stunned.

That is the humanbeing, the Dukebeing. Why is this one here now? Is it teaching us, as well? No, there is little of the Music in this humanbeing.

The Music of the Spheres. You know little about this mysterious power, the science of the mind taken to almost magical levels. Those trained in the Music can create light, bolts of energy from their hands, or beautiful illusions—or destroy objects and enslave minds. Few in the galaxy have mastered it.

In the Kakklakks, it seems, Duke Carabajal has found a hive-mind capable of using the Music of the Spheres, and he's had his Musicians train it as the Domain's secret weapon—the Subverter. From what you know of the Music, it's easy to understand how Zygash was turned into a loyal servant of the Domain. This Subverter has to be stopped, or the Resistance is done for!

"What are you?" is your sensible first question, and you have many more. The hive-mind tells you much.

The Kakklakks (you learn) are a very long-lived race who have inhabited asteroids in this system since before humans spread across the galaxy. The Kakklakks raise the "cattle," the large buglike creatures, feeding on their fluids. The cattle dine on fungus that the Kakklakks harvest elsewhere in the asteroid.

The species developed certain proficiencies in the Music of the Spheres to aid in contacting other asteroid colonies, so they could reproduce. One hive is unable to reproduce on its own; when two hives meet, every million or so orbits, they join, die, and thereby create new hives.

The Domain only recently discovered their nature. When Duke Carabajal learned of the hive's use of the Music, he had his most trusted Musicians begin training it toward his own ends. He found that although the hive lacked several important abilities in the Music, it had achieved proficiency far beyond human levels in mind control.

The hive-mind, now code-named "the Subverter," will soon begin possessing the minds of selected Resistance leaders across the galaxy. It began with Zygash.

"Why Gash?"

That otherbeing is less alien to us than the bizarre, deformed humanbeings. It gave us useful exercise.

Somehow you have to keep this thing from menacing the Resistance. Running away is useless; you have to confront the Subverter, either persuading, intimidating, or killing it.

Killing the Subverter sounds like a pretty swell idea, until you examine the situation. You have a blaster; it has a horde of separate bodies with mean-looking mandibles. You picture the battle in your mind: You let loose with red bolts of energy; the Subverter screams, and the pile dissolves into dozens of individual survivors; they leap at you.

You could pick many of them out of the air, and blow others away as they land on you, but their numbers would bear you to the cavern floor, and that would be the last you knew.

You can't throw your life away here; too many others are counting on you. (There's a switch from your old smuggling days! Maybe this Resistance business is changing you.) You search your thoughts for some way to defeat this Subverter.

If you try bribing the Subverter, go to 72.

If you offer the gravball tournament holo-tapes, go to 49.

If you appeal to the Subverter's honor, charity, or sense of freedom, go to 48.

If you threaten the Subverter, go to 91.

81

"You'll pardon me if I doubt your sincerity, Jorth," you say, pulling him toward the freighter. The little governor fights like a ferocious jaggro, shouting "No, it's true! We can't survive if you take that junkheap!"

The vigor of his struggle catches you by surprise. You can hardly hold on! How did this little creep get so strong? you wonder. But you have leverage on him. You get him in a sleeper hold, and after a few routine threats on both sides, he calms down.

Gash bypasses the freighter's crude security measures in moments, and you head for the gangway with Jorth in tow. At that moment a tremendous shock jolts the stronghold. A ship nearby collapses in a pile of twisted metal and smoke. You duck and grab for the gangway's support. When you look up, Jorth is gone.

Looking into the haze of smoke, you decide it's not worth going after him. You'll be off the stronghold before he can do anything, anyway. All are aboard that are going aboard. You begin an emergency launch sequence to blast away from the sinking *Ocean Lord*.

Go to 3.

82

In the cavernous customs building, a generic building like a hundred others on a hundred other worlds, you wait in line with the other tourists. When your turn comes, you give a false identity and cover story as you have hundreds of times in the past. "Nazzen Dreen's my name, beverage export's my game. Scouting out new flavors for Dreenco's upcoming line of Planet Colas. Different cola from each planet in a system, get it? Bet you got lots of exotic seafood here on—where am I this time? Pellaj?—that could be the next flavored soda sensation."

There's a tight moment when an inspector asks why you don't have any luggage. "Can you believe it?" you reply. "The spaceline misread the destination label and routed my bags through Pollar, not Pellaj! They're probably halfway to Ganndro by now."

The inspector surveys you coolly. Finally he says, "Yeah, we see a lot of that."

Go to 41.

83

You signal to the robots and loaderbots outside the ship. "Clear the hangar," you tell them from the gangway. "I'm undertaking a little unscheduled demolition."

"Pardon, sir?" says the robot foreman.

"Just clear out," you repeat. "Wrench, get aboard!"

"Yes, sir." The robot wheels up the gangway. "Are you planning massive mayhem, Captain Hayl?"

"Couldn't have put it better myself." You close the hatch. The engines are powering up, the eDrive purring, and all is right with the world. A voice comes over the radio: "Maintenance crew, this is Central. We're picking up power surges in your hangar. What is your condition, over?"

"Ahh, condition?" you say, monitoring the core temperatures. Another few moments. . . . "Um, what sort of condition do you mean? We're doing fine, really. Or is that what you meant by condition?" You glimpse the robots outside. They're rolling to the exit, but then peering back in from the doorway.

"Where's the power coming from? Who is this?"

The console glows green. You think about a grand exit line: The power comes from freedom, haha!— This is the voice of the Resistance, down with the Domain! But it's just not your style.

With a terse "We'll talk about it later," you switch off the radio, hit the shields, trigger the top blaster pod, and blow a huge hole in the roof of the hangar.

Alarms squawk, and the robots shy back from the doorway. The *Prosperogenesis* shakes as the rubble bounces off the shields. "Come on, baby, more firepower!" you shout. More bolts of energy rip into the stone roof, and all at once the ceiling caves in. Starlight shines through from outside. "Go!" you shout to nobody in particular (or maybe to the ship itself), and you push the throttle to full.

The bottom blaster pod takes care of some stone outcroppings with a few tight shots. The *Genesis* soars out into space above the asteroid, engines roaring. Below, pandemonium reigns. None of the colony's heavy weapons have come to bear on you; they weren't ready for an attack from within!

You emerge at the edge of the mining base. With a tight bend, you sweep around and down so that the whole complex stretches beneath you. The buildings are arranged in a series of spokes radiating from a central generator tower. On this side of the tower, you see the main landing and maintenance area. Its underground bays are starting to open up to space, revealing a squadron of Domain spacecraft. They're scrambling, and should be up and flying in a moment.

If you let them, that is. You swoop down at high speed, dodging the ineffective blaster cannons mounted over each bay. They're sitting targets, lined up in your sights. Even hampered by the remote controls, you have no trouble hitting every ship in the line. They blow up before they can lift off, and bay doors splinter into shards from the explosions.

You pull away and bend back to the generating tower. "Try shooting me here!" you yell at the blaster embankments surrounding the base. "Just try it!" But as you expected, they can't risk shooting at the tower. One miss could blow the station into deep space.

You have a moment to wonder what's next. The answer comes as three undamaged ships zoom down from overhead. They must have been on patrol elsewhere in the asteroid belt. Bad luck! Now, the success of your entire mission depends on the sure touch of your fingers on that remote control.

Well, at least they're using standard Domain tactics, splitting up to try an envelope crossfire. Resistance piloting seminars give standard evasion tactics against the Envelope—and you taught those seminars! You sideslip toward one ship near the station tower, skirt a silvery conning dish, send a blaster bolt toward the most distant ship. It dodges easily, but the crossfire pattern falls apart. In the even shootout with the near ship, your superior skill tells. A bolt strikes its stabilizer, sparks fly, and it spins away helplessly into the starry sky. One down.

The second bears down from the high point of the Envelope, while the far ship comes back into formation. Time for evasive action. Whipping in a tight one-eighty around the generating tower, you wind up at half your previous altitude. The pilots never expected this maneuver, because no one but a maniac would try it. You reinforce this impression by laughing maniacally as you blast them both in the underbodies!

One ship actually manages an ugly but survivable crash landing not far from the mine. But the last Domain ship, engine sputtering fire, spirals down, bounces off the generator tower, and plows into a row of mine buildings. A line of explosions springs up. Great shooting!

Now you have to get by the perimeter defenses. Spiralling around the power generator, you're safe for the moment—but you know what will happen should you fly clear of it.

That gives you a crazy idea. Triggering your blaster pods in tandem, you fire twin lines of energy at the tower, from bottom to top and back down again. Gouts of flame erupt. The tower trembles, and a shiver runs its length. Any moment now, it should blow.

You hope to ride the crest of the explosion away from Dvaad, avoiding the blasts of the perimeter weapons. *Sort of like setting off a bomb in my back pocket to launch myself over a fence*, you think.

Ready to time the run to a split instant, you ride the controls hard. Any moment now—

Suddenly you hear a voice in your mind: *Humanbeing, we do not allow this.*

Images and commands fill your awareness. A writhing pile of insects—

Run the ship into the ground, comes the command.

—a vast, ancient, absolutely alien intellect—

You cannot harm the Domain.

—a glimpse of Duke Carabajal's Musicians instructing this pupil, the "Subverter," in certain chords of the Music—

You must repent and sacrifice yourself.

It's the natives, a hive-mind! You're pushing down on the attitude controls, sending the *Genesis* plunging toward the ground and certain destruction. This is what happened to Gash! The Resistance can't stand against it!

You struggle to break free. The battle is in your mind, but you sweat and strain as though pitted against a physical opponent. You're fighting against your own body!

Sacrifice yourself—yes—no! There are too many others who depend on you now. Your friends in the Resistance have risked their lives for you, many times, and you would do it for them—for these are your friends in mind and spirit, and have a greater hold on you than any alien mind can muster.

You hit the blaster trigger for one final burst, then zoom high and away as the generator tower explodes. The fireball is big, painfully bright, and hot enough to scorch your thrusters. Pulling away, you see the explosions multiply, feel the overlapping shockwaves that take out the base, the perimeter blasters, and every living thing on Dvaad. As though bands snap from your mind, your thoughts are your own once more.

You're free of the Subverter, and so is the Resistance. You're ready to leave Dvaad.

If you have already gone to Pellaj, go to 93.
If you have not yet gone to Pellaj, go to 67.

84

When you and Wrench wander around Dvaad, most of it seems like just another mine: muffled explosions underground, winding tunnels with gravsled rails along the ceiling, dim light, mist on the ground, and the usual crew of robots and administrators. You easily lose yourself in the crowd, walking freely in the very throat of a Domain operation.

"This place is so ordinary it's suspicious," you say to Wrench, thinking aloud. "Why would the Domain bother with this little operation?"

"I have no idea, sir. I'm just a robot."

The only unusual feature is the local life-form, a stubby white insectlike thing with a hard, ridged shell and too many legs. Now and then one wanders by, making *chik-chuk* sounds and clicking its mandibles. None of them reach higher than your knee. No one pays these natives any attention.

"You!" shouts a voice behind you. "No one permitted in this area! What's your authority?" Now you notice this area is different: Laboratory robots carry advanced research devices, and the whole tunnel has a clean, antiseptic odor. Here in this mine, you've found a Domain research lab. And a uniformed technician has found you.

You look him over. Slender, unarmed, and officious; you grin. All it takes is a couple of punches. Dragging the unconscious form behind a stack of oxygen tanks, you notice a lounge area nearby. A perfect spot to find some leads to the *Genesis*.

You have a nice new tech jacket to pull over your own black vest. You put it on—hmm. Not exactly your size. Oh, well, the black vest is okay, though it could use cleaning after what you've been through. You enter the lounge.

It's small, shiny, and spartan. Two off-duty technicians rest on a divan. They watch a holo of a gravball tournament. With their doughy, expressionless faces, they hardly look smart enough to be techs. "Hi!" you begin, picking a cover story suited to the audience. "I'm Delbert Lorfin, researcher for the Galactic Encyclopedia. Mind if I ask you fellows some questions?"

They come to their feet. "Uh—Encyclopedia?" asks one.

"You know, the big Galactic Encyclopedia project. Information on worlds, races, societies, economics and politics, technology? Big foundation set up at the other end of the galaxy? You *must* have heard of it!"

"Uhh. Yes!" says one, and the other takes the cue. "Yes, I've heard about it. Yes. What can we do for you?"

You've won them over, but it turns out they don't know much. A G12 Marauder XX ship was brought in some time back. According to their directions, you can find the ship by going out the door and turning left. You ask delicately about "big new projects," but their lips close tight as airlocks.

After you ask a few questions, they leave to return to work. You stay to look around. There's not much of interest here. Furniture, some snack food, lots of gravball tournament tapes. On a hunch, you take the pocket holo-player and a few tapes.

Suddenly you hear voices outside. "Kavel! Somebody's hurt Kavel!" They've found the tech you slugged. They probably won't believe that's standard practice for a Galactic Encyclopedia researcher. You have to get out—

Nope, too late. Three soldiers appear at the lounge doorway. You pull your blaster and blow a hole in the jamb, sending them back for cover. What a place for a fight!

You haven't a chance if you try to hold your ground. Searching for a way out, you notice the back entrance to the lounge. Beyond lies a dark tunnel. Fleeing like a terrified Alharutian wingsnake is, for Rogan Hayl, the work of a moment.

You run down the tunnel into the wilder areas beyond the mining colony. Mist rises around your feet, and the walls contort into twisting passages untouched by humanity. Finally you slow down to a walk and look around.

Go to 80.

85

As suddenly as an acid missile's explosion, the entire stronghold jolts with fierce tremors. While the floor shakes, you hold tightly to your precious hostage. Jorth blubbers, too frightened to try to escape.

Another shock, and then another. The floor cracks, and a stream of salty water gushes up to soak the floor. Below, you hear the rumbling bellow of Cetapods—lots of them.

"It's a raid!" the soldiers shout. Now you understand what's happened: The Cetapods are attacking the *Ocean Lord* to free their leader! And that means—

"Gash! Let's blast!" you shout, pulling Jorth along by his collar. The troopers stand helpless while you, the G'rax, and Wrench leave the chamber and enter the chaos of a sinking city. "*Grrrrnnnnhhhgaaah!*" cries Gash.

"Good idea! Which way?" You follow Gash's lead through the corridor toward the spaceport, while hundreds of technicians, troopers, and bureaucrats rush by in both directions. You hear cracks and explosions, nearby and in the distance. Passing an atrium, you see a gigantic black muzzle thrust upward through the ferrocrete floor, spraying rubble and water everywhere.

Through a window you see a Cetapod leaping up from the sea, impressively higher with each second, water streaming away from its flanks. More and more of the body appears, towering like a cruiser in dry dock. Finally the flanged tail's powerful strokes drive the entire creature free of the water. For a breath it hangs suspended in air, then falls—hard—on a dome of the stronghold. The supports snap with sharp cracks, and the Cetapod dives straight through the floor back into the ocean.

They'll take the whole place down before long, you think as you shove through the crowded corridors. Jorth doesn't struggle; he must want to get out as badly as you do. Luckily no pursuit could possibly trace you through this confusion.

Gash guides you to the landing field and docking yard. There you find an array of spacecraft rocking gently with the tremors of the sinking city. Nothing looks ready for liftoff except a grimy gas freighter with obsolete attitude thrusters. Shrugging, you pull Jorth toward it.

"No! No, Hayl, we'll never get off the ground in that old trap!" says Jorth shrilly. "Listen, Hayl, I have my own yacht at the other end of the yard. I keep it fueled and ready for departure all the time, in case of attack. Listen, Hayl!"

You're listening, but you don't necessarily believe him. A space yacht would be much better than this jalopy, but Jorth may be leading you into a trap.

If you follow Jorth to the other end of the yard, go to 50.

If you take the freighter, go to 81.

86

You fly to the coordinates for the Resistance base, not far from the floating stronghold. Then, holding your breath, you pilot the *Rustbucket* straight down into the sea. And there's no suspense; it immediately begins leaking from every seam.

In the enormous coral reef nearby, you can clearly see the entrance to an interior chamber. But the very fact that it isn't camouflaged tells you beyond doubt that the base is deserted. The Resistance routinely switches locations.

You have no time to wonder about your next step, because you're ankle-deep in water. You wonder if the ship will make it back to the surface—but you don't wonder for long. When you give it some throttle, the engines go dead. The cabin walls bulge inward with deep groans, and the leaks become gushers.

"Captain Hayl," says Wrench calmly, "we're about to be horribly drowned."

"Thanks for the news. Bail out, quick!"

Fortunately, the ship has an emergency sea-skimmer with room for both you and Wrench. Probably every ship within bailout distance of Pellaj has a skimmer as standard equipment. You wrestle it to the airlock by its handlebars, check the bubble hood for leaks, make sure the jets are powered, and cycle through to the sea outside. You emerge underwater just as the *Rustbucket* collapses, beyond hope of repair.

A nice fix. Unpowered, the skimmer floats to the surface. You straddle its seat, wondering what to do. The stronghold *Ocean Lord* is on the horizon. Do you dare approach it?

You don't get time to think about it. As soon as you break the surface, six high wakes turn toward you. You look around at the distant buzz, to find you've been spotted by a Domain patrol.

"Captain Hayl, if those soldiers catch us—"

"Shut up, Wrench." You twist the skimmer's right handlebar, and its engine's buzz rises in pitch. You speed away from the patrol. The chase is on!

After a few moments it becomes clear the patrol is closing on you. Muttering curses in Galactic Standard and in the secret language of your G'rax Reverence Line, you look across the open ocean for something, anything, to use against them. Not far from the Domain stronghold you make out a line of foam— rocky shoals. A reef. Well, better than nothing.

As you near the reef, you make out many bright colors and strange textures. The crash of the surf is the only sound besides the wind whipping past you and the buzz of your engine. To cross the shallows, you send your skimmer skipping like a rock over the shoals. Every landing sends a jet of spray shooting behind you, and every new jump threatens to shake you loose.

Two soldiers crash magnificently on the shoals behind you, but four are still chasing you.

On these shoals, you and your seat become distant acquaintances. Stony growths scrape at the skimmer's underbody. Suddenly, from a shallow area something bursts out of the water. You don't see it for long, but it has lots of spines and bright spots and makes a noise like *Oogaloobooah!* Startled, you lose your grip.

Splash! Off you go, into the shallows. The sharp coral cuts at you. Fortunately, your skimmer careens to a smooth stop nearby, with Wrench still aboard. "Captain Hayl, my data banks show that some small Pellajian predators secrete acid dangerous to equipment. That one you found just now, for instance—"

"Not now, Wrench!"

You regain your feet in seconds, but the Domain soldiers are too close for you to run or swim. Standing alone, on foot, against four approaching skimmers, you feel like the circus jackrobats of Pollux Nine, who face down charging Hargrogs with no weapon but a sash of cloth.

Fortunately, your blaster works slightly better than a sash—especially in your hands. At six years old in the Carelax desert, you could hit the tiniest bloodflies with thrown rocks, and you've only gotten better over the years. Your blasts unerringly strike the lead skimmers' hoods and engines. The troopers are flung back from the handlebars, and the uncontrolled skimmers plow into the reef.

The explosions almost knock you down, and the last two Domain soldiers veer away to escape the fireball. Coral crunches beneath your boot-heels as you run clumsily over the reef. You reach your skimmer.

"I'm happy to report that I prevented possible acid damage, Captain Hayl. If I hadn't been here, you might have been in real trouble."

Ignoring Wrench, you rev up the skimmer again. Too late! The enemy skimmers are so close it's hopeless. Again you reach for your blaster, knowing that this time they're ready for you.

The two enemy skimmers suddenly explode out of the water straight up, and twin blasts deafen you! The soldiers fly off their skimmers and fall to the reef, where they lie unmoving. Foamy water showers down for long seconds afterward. What happened?

Then you understand. A wing of skimmers rises to the surface beyond the reef. Their pilots flash Resistance hand signals. You wanted to contact the Resistance on Pellaj; looks like they've contacted you, and just in time!

They ground on the reef and greet you politely. "Heard you were headed our way, Hayl," says one. "We were supposed to look out for you."

You grin. "I wish everyone looked out for me the way you folks do. You used grenades?"

"One for each skimmer. We don't usually like to use them, because it damages the reef. Speaking of that, let's move off, and we'll lead you to the base."

In your skimmer, you and Wrench follow the Resistance team across a stretch of open water. Then, on their signal, you all pilot the skimmers down under the surface and through green emptiness. A long whalelike shape in the distance grows larger, larger—a Cetapod, one of the Pellajian natives. The twin clusters of tentacles on its sloping head signal to the approaching skimmers. Each tentacle is big enough to swipe the entire wing of skimmers out of the ocean, but the creature only waits calmly.

As you begin to wonder where the base is, the creature opens its mouth. The water rushes inward, sweeping the skimmers ahead of you straight into the creature's mouth! You stare in horror—then in shock, as the last pilot in line waves for you to follow!

"Captain Hayl," says Wrench, "is this some kind of ceremony that organic beings use to test each other's courage?"

You look blankly at the colossal mouth. It still hangs open before you. You could reverse thrust on the skimmer and escape the fate of those Resistance fighters. But they didn't look afraid or even upset. . . .

"If it's a test of courage," you tell Wrench, speaking loud enough to drown out the pounding of your heart, "then, by the galaxy, I'm going to pass it!"

And you pilot the skimmer straight into the Cetapod's mouth!

Go to 6.

87

Your second appeal is more desperate than the first. "Gash, think of the Resistance! They're all counting on you to break out of this!"

But like the first, it's useless. The blaster bolt hits

you squarely, knocking you down.

You knew you didn't have a chance. Lying there, seeing the G'rax loom above you, seeing him prepare the killing stroke, you barely whisper, "How will you ever get along without me, buddy?"

Gash pauses. He stands motionless, while Jorth and the troops urge him to strike. A low growl escapes him: "*Hrrnngh.*"

Your eyes widen. He's back! He's all right!

And now, you realize as new energy flows through your limbs, you both have a chance to escape.

Go to 14.

88

Awfully plush for a prison, you think as you look around Baron Jorth's headquarters. There are over-stuffed divans upholstered in animal hide, and feather plumes arranged in expensive vases. Floating globes create a dim light, and the air carries a burning smell of incense. Even the floor you're lying on is richly carpeted.

But there's nothing exotic about the Elite Imperial Soldiers guarding you. Blaster rifles surround you, and your own blaster and possessions are gone. Wrench the robot stands helpless behind a line of soldiers.

"You are not to think of escape, Captain Hayl," purrs a voice from the shadows. Cradled in a velvet bodychair sits the Domain governor of this world, Baron Jorth. Pale, fat as a slathorp, with small narrow eyes and a large wide mouth, Jorth smirks at you. "I have power of life and death over you, Hayl. You will not consider escaping."

He scratches at his uniform. The standard dark blue Domain jacket hangs unbuttoned over Jorth's belly. Underneath it he wears a tunic of song-serpent scales, a conspicuous luxury. And what are those strange bulges at his shoulders and elbows? You have no time to wonder, for Jorth speaks again.

If you have already visited Dvaad, go to 59.
If you have not been to Dvaad yet, go to 42.

89

Dodging past the orbital sentries around Pellaj, you don't wish for any ship but the *Prosperogenesis* under you. Despite all it's gone through, the G12 Marauder XX handles like a dream. But you can't head for Baron Jorth's *Ocean Lord* stronghold directly, because the Domains will spot your ship at once. So: the subtle approach. Hope the waterproofing is still okay. . . .

The *Genesis* dives into clear bluish water, trailing bubbles. With your state-of-the-art shielded communications gear, you can contact the Resistance without fear of detection. "Tandon Rey, do you copy?" you call, naming the local Resistance commander. "Tandon Rey, it's Rogan Hayl, talk to me."

A pause, some clicks and static, then: "Tandon Rey here. We've fixed your position and verified your ship codes, Hayl. You check out."

"Gee, thanks. Efficient operation you've got there."

"We expected you, once we learned your G'rax buddy came here to join the Domain."

"He didn't join the Domain!" you shout, for what seems the hundredth time. "He was brainwashed by a Domain weapon called the Subverter. I took care of the Subverter on Dvaad, so Gash should be okay now."

"If you call being a prisoner of Baron Jorth 'okay,' " says Tandon. "I'm not even going to try to talk you out of a rescue mission. Check in at our base before you do anything headstrong. We'll outfit you and set you up. Wait until you see the new base, you'll never guess where it is—"

Wham! The ship rolls to one side and you grab for the console. What happened? You see the explanation out the viewport: A Cetapod has slammed into the *Genesis!* You've never seen one before, but when it's as big as two buildings and has a flanged tail (that's about to tear your ship open), what else could it be?

You thought the Cetapods were friendly to the Resistance, but there's no time for speculation. You hit the reverse throttle on the *Genesis* instrument panel, even as that tail sweeps back toward you, filling the viewport. . . .

Skirting around the upper flange of the tail, you zoom straight backward at top acceleration. The Cetapod grows smaller. It shows no interest in pursuing

you. You almost believe it doesn't see you.

Your experiences in the Resistance have taught you to think before acting. You tie in the *Genesis*'s public address loudhailer and speak. "Hi, don't hit me again," you say, hearing your words echo through the water outside. "Don't hit me, don't swallow me, don't pound me into the sea floor. Please."

The Cetapod turns with slow strokes of its tail. The current jostles the *Genesis* like a blaster bolt. One great eye heaves into view, a very human-looking eye. It meets your own, and widens in, what, amazement?

The creature's huge mouth opens. "*Thossolorithossa salarith*," it says in a booming voice so deep you can barely hear it. You can't understand it, but from the way the Cetapod swims carefully away, you get the impression it apologized for brushing against you.

"Hayl, come in, do you copy?" says Tandon Rey over the console speaker.

"Just chatting with a native." When he hears your story, he's convinced the Cetapod just overlooked you. "Anything smaller than a Morione Cruiser looks kind of shrimpy to them," he says, laughing. You force yourself to laugh politely with him, then get directions to his position.

You dock, lower the gangplank and study the strange new Resistance base.

Go to 6.

90

You give the soldier your password. He nods and steps aside as the door slides back. You saunter through—and drop from a blow to the base of your skull. As you slide into unconsciousness, you realize that your password must have been a plant to catch

Resistance fighters like you.

You wake up as a prisoner of Baron Jorth.

Go to 88.

91

"Listen, bug-brain," you say, "I have many power-ful friends who will be very angry if you destroy the Resistance, or even try to hurt me for that matter. Resistance fighters, platoons of them! The *entire Resistance fleet* is waiting not far from here, and I can call in a strike force with a snap of my fingers." You hold your fingers poised to snap.

The Subverter appears impressed. *This is disturbing news the humanbeing brings. We must survive to breed above all else. We will eliminate this threat at once.* The pile dissolves as dozens of individual natives move toward you, mandibles clacking.

"Uh—hey, wait, don't get me wrong—there are people waiting to hear from me, you know—" But the natives cannot understand your words anymore.

You unholster your blaster and fire. Fire everywhere, to the left and right, even near your own feet, for the insects are crawling on your legs. You whirl back and forth, frantic, firing again, and the odor of burning bugs fills the cave. The insects fall, screeching, by the dozens, but they outnumber the bolts in your blaster.

When the charge readout hits zero, you grab the weapon by the barrel and use it as a hammer, but still the insects keep coming. The fight is hopeless. Though you struggle valiantly and finally defend yourself with hands and feet, you eventually fall. The cattle bugs will eat well now. Your adventure is over.

The End

92

What password will you give?

"Approach vector"? Go to 90.
"Fusion furnace"? Go to 76.
Make something up? Go to 69.

93

At the helm of the *Genesis*, your best friend Zygash at your side, you blast off from Pellaj for a new Resistance mission. You make the jump to eSpace, and . . .

Twenty standard days later, Scion Duke Carabajal walks with a confident stride into his immense Axis Sanctum, at the core of the Carabajal Chateau-Station. The orbital palace is built around this long tube, like an ancient smokestack surrounded by rank upon rank of spheres, spires, and gleaming fins.

Carabajal looks down and sees the forest world of Bryson. The Duke's voice echoes in the Sanctum. "Bryson is beautiful tonight," he comments to his sentry, looking down.

"Yes, Your Excellency," says the sentry.

Gravity generators give a "top" and "bottom" to the tube. Here at the bottom, the Duke has made his Axis Sanctum. The floor is made of clear plastoid, shot through with lines of greenish light. A walker in the Axis Sanctum seems to float on a lattice of light with black space beneath. The beautiful station stays perpetually aligned so that the planet Bryson hangs huge and green below, while the system's sun shines down the smokestack from exactly overhead. Filters turn its light a dim blue.

No furniture mars the open expanse of the lattice, save for a desk and chairs of hull metal. Carabajal and the sentry walk toward the desk, their footsteps echoing high above. Exotic creatures and insects from all the worlds in this sector fly overhead.

Carabajal looks as vigorous as those animals. The clan ruler was once known for stuttering speech, an old man's speech, full of hesitation and repetition. Lately, however, he has been speaking in a strangely youthful baritone, in rapid, sure sentences. His smooth skin has a peculiar flat tone to it, like a mask. He moves like a man thirty years his junior.

At the desk Carabajal punches a button, and on a panel an unlabeled spot lights up violet. Apparently he ignores it. He glances at the nearby sentry. "Soldier, that weapon needs cleaning."

"Yes, Your Excellency," says the sentry, his voice muffled by his armor's visor.

"Let me see it." The Duke takes the blaster rifle casually, checks the charge, thumbs off the safety, then abruptly shoulders it and points it directly at the sentry!

"Don't move," says Carabajal. "Take off that visor."

"How can I take off the visor when I'm not supposed to move?" says the sentry.

"Hayl!"

You slowly remove the visor and stare into Duke Carabajal's eyes. "I have to hand it to you, Duke. Who would have thought you had a scanner in that desk?"

"A routine precaution." He backs up, holding the rifle steady, and stabs another button. "It also has a silent alarm. Hayl, I must thank you. Most of my forces throughout this sector have had priority orders to capture you, even before you destroyed the *Ocean Lord* and the Subverter. Now, having evaded them all, you casually walk into my own stronghold. Why?"

"I need to know, Carabajal. I know you wanted me; you subverted Zygash and took my ship so that I'd give myself up to you. Why? Why did you want me captured alive? Why do you look so young?"

"All three questions have the same answer: rejuvenation! You are one of dozens of specimens my scientists have located on many different worlds. Some have advanced intellect, others great strength. You have amazing reflexes and marksmanship. My technicians have learned how to copy my victims' relevant physical systems and implant them in my body. Unfortunately, the copying process destroys the original body. A small sacrifice, relatively speaking. Their contributions have made me a man of thirty, of twenty!"

"They've made you a maniac, if you weren't already," you say. "Thanks. I had to know."

Carabajal smiles thinly. "You are the last target left on my list, and I thank you for turning yourself over."

"Not exactly," you tell him. You turn around and walk toward the exit.

"Halt! Make no mistake, Hayl, I shall shoot. I can hit you without much damaging your nervous system. That is the only part of you I require."

"I'm not done with it," you say. You keep walking.

The Duke fires. The rifle clicks. Nothing happens.

"By the way," you say, almost at the door, "I fiddled with that rifle's charge readout. It's empty."

"Guards! Soldiers!" Carabajal shouts.

"There aren't any."

He stares dumbly. "Aren't—?"

"Since we entered this room, the Resistance has controlled every person on this station. Your guards are being evacuated to the lifeboats."

The Duke still stares.

"You know, Duke, that Dvaad asteroid mine is one of about, oh, eight billion asteroids in that belt. Did you think there was only one Kakklakk colony there? Those bugs live everywhere in the belt."

Carabajal speaks barely above a whisper, but you can read his lips: "Oh, no."

"The Musicians in the Resistance found another colony. In return for various inducements I won't go into, the hive-mind joined us and has just started some Subverting of its own. Once the station is evacuated, we'll knock it out of orbit and let it burn up in the atmosphere. I assume that you'll follow clan etiquette and go down with your ship."

You turn and walk out the door. For all his youth and vigor, the Duke stands helplessly.

A short time later, from the cockpit of the *Prospero-genesis*, you watch the Chateau-Station's beautiful, glorious fireball streaking across the face of Bryson. It vaporizes long before it would hit the surface.

"*Hnnnaraaagh hraaa-anngh*," says Gash.

"I wonder too," you answer. "Both the Domain and the Resistance have a much bigger weapon now. It's a weapon that could turn on us both. I hope the Kakklakks never get it in their collective mind to take over the galaxy.

"Well. We've got missions to do, buddy. Set course for Akinas. Maybe that baron has bought some more Babannian mood crystals worth stealing."

The End